$3.95
g

THE RED TOWERS OF GRANADA

The Red Towers of Granada

GEOFFREY
TREASE , 1409.

Illustrated by

CHARLES KEEPING

NEW YORK
THE VANGUARD PRESS, INC.

Library of Congress Catalog Card Number: 67-18646

Copyright, ©, mcmlxvi, by Geoffrey Trease

Manufactured in the United States of America

Contents

CHAPTER ONE

Dead or Alive?

IT is a strange and terrible thing to listen to one's own funeral service.

All these years later, every detail is clear. It burns in my memory like a fresh brand.

The church flagstones, cold even at midsummer, press hard under my aching kneecaps. The mustiness of the old black pall is in my nostrils: it has been stretched over the two trestles, which usually take the coffin. But for me there is no coffin, of course, and I crouch there as I have been told, between the trestles, under that stifling cloth, in front of the altar.

Dimly I see Father Simon moving to and fro. His voice drones on. I am one of the few people in the village who can follow the Latin words. The others — family, friends, neighbours — understand only that something awful is being enacted. I catch the faint murmur and rustle, the strangled sobs and whispers of comfort, the movement as folk make the sign of the cross.

All this is still as vivid as on the day it happened. Even now it returns in my dreams and I wake sweating with the horror of it.

'My son, the time has come . . .'

Father Simon loomed over me. He spoke in English and I realised that the service was ended. He was stripping off his vestments. There was compassion in his voice.

That only brought home to me more poignantly the dreadfulness of my situation.

Father Simon had never liked me since he came to our parish when the old priest died. He resented me in some strange way, because our former parson had picked me out and sent me for schooling at the monastery.

I would rather he had spoken to me as he usually did. This new gentleness was eerie. It was the tone in which people spoke of the dead.

Dazed with the nightmare of it all, I crawled from under the black cloth, made my reverence towards the altar, and stumbled down the aisle. To right and left the great round pillars seemed to reel and sway. Pale faces peered forward, then shrank back.

A doomed prisoner walks chained, between guards, or is dragged to the scaffold on a hurdle, bumping over the cobbles. But I, no less doomed, walked freely towards the arched patch of daylight cut by the open door.

No man laid a finger on me. No man dared. But they all crept after me, keeping their distance, stealthy and murmurous as a midnight tide.

The sun was shining outside, the birds chirping gaily. It was like any ordinary summer morning.

I stood there, blinking. I looked down at myself. I took in, for the first time, the strange clothes they had made me put on: the hooded cloak, the ox-hide boots worn over slippers of fur. . . . And I saw my hands, with the dry discoloured patches that had caused everything.

Father Simon faced me. He took his stand two or three paces distant. The length of a man's grave.

He was not a bad man, our parson. But he was proud and obstinate and self-important. He liked to be the only man in the village who knew anything. And because he really had very little learning he resented me. Not only could I read and write but I had been two years in the schools at Oxford. When I came home in the summer to help with haymaking and harvest, I read the wariness — the fear, almost — in those red-rimmed eyes.

His own work he knew well enough, I give him that. On this fatal morning he had primed himself with all the rules that were laid down. Everything was properly and decently done.

'Listen, Robert.' He called me Robert, though I am known always as Robin.

'Yes, Father?'

'Listen carefully. You must not enter a church again, a tavern or a bakehouse, a market or any assembly of people.'

'No, Father.'

'You must not drink from any stream except with a cup. You must not wash yourself or your belongings in any stream.'

'No, Father.'

'Or walk barefoot. Or speak to healthy folk. We have made you this clapper so that you can give warning as you go.' He pointed to where it lay on the grass, just two pieces of wood joined by a leather thong. With it were the cup, knife and plate that I was entitled to. I stooped and picked them up.

'You are free to go where you will,' he continued. Free, I thought! But I bit back the acid comment that sprang to my lips. 'You will find a hospital at Blyth, or you can go south to St Leonard's at Nottingham. We cannot make you go to any hospital — but how else can you live? You cannot go back to Oxford. I shall send word to Merton College, so that another scholar can have your place. You understand?'

'I understand.'

3

I knew that he was only doing his duty. It was the usual thing for the priest to examine cases like mine, to decide upon them, and make a report.

Then Father Simon did the last terrible symbolic act laid down by the rules of the Church.

He took a spade which someone handed to him, thrust it into a little heap of freshly turned earth, and cast the soil over my feet as I stood.

'Be thou dead to the world,' he pronounced solemnly, 'but alive again unto God.'

The crowd muttered Amen and crossed themselves. I heard my mother scream and saw her start forward as if to put her arms round me. My father and my uncles took hold of her and dragged her back.

It was best to go as quickly as possible. I pulled the cowl forward over my head and went down the path.

The crowd parted hastily. Most of them avoided my eyes. Only one old enemy faced me gloating, a lout I had once beaten in a rough-and-tumble. 'Where's your grin today?' he demanded.

I took no notice of him. What really hurt was when I came to the gate of the churchyard and a girl stood there among her friends, the girl we had fought over. She looked at me, and I saw the utter revulsion in her face. She turned away. She could not manage even a word of farewell.

Father Simon was at my heels with final words of admonishment. 'Worship God and give Him thanks. Have patience and the Lord will be with thee. Amen.'

But there were no thanks on my trembling lips as I took my lonely, doomed way into the world.

CHAPTER TWO

A Man in a Yellow Cap

THEY say it is a great sin to wish yourself dead. If you had been in my shoes would you not have been tempted?

It had all happened so quickly, I was still numbed by the blow that had been struck me.

Two days ago I had been joking and laughing with my friends in the hayfield, only a little troubled by those unsightly blotches on my skin. I had put them down to the rough work in the sunshine after a year huddled in chilly University halls, listening to lectures and handling no tool but a quill.

Then I had become suddenly aware of looks and whispers, of people edging away, of old friends refusing a swig of ale from my mug. Father Simon had been called.

5

He had peered at me, careful not to touch. He had given his judgement.

I had a sickness for which no man knew a cure. I had leprosy. I was unclean. I must be cast out. That was the teaching of the Church.

Once the doom was spoken there had been no delay. I had slept that last night — tried to sleep, rather — in the village that had always been my home. Because of the fine midsummer weather I had lain outside our cottage, where I could do no more harm.

And this morning they had held this grotesque kind of funeral ceremony for one who still lived and breathed and felt much the same — shock apart — as he had done two days earlier. It was called the Office for the Seclusion of Lepers. I had never thought to have a priest say it over me.

Yet it had happened. It had been real, no nightmare. Somehow I had to take it in, come to terms with my affliction.

The last cottage, the common, the duck pond, lay behind me. The great field too, with the grassy boundary stripes green against the paie gold of the ripening barley . . .

The road stretched in front, grey, dusty, empty. Just like my own future, I thought, with a wry twist of the lips.

The edge of the forest was near. I plunged gladly into its leafy gloom. I had always loved Sherwood. Its whispers were friendly, very different from the whispers of men. It was a hiding-place, and at that moment a hiding place was all I wanted.

I do not know how many hours I walked. My instinct was to put as many miles as possible between myself and home. Whether to turn north or south, seek charity at a lepers' hospital or stay in the wilderness like an animal, were questions I still could not consider. I trudged straight along the road, but my reeling mind went in circles.

Westwood lies in a little world of its own, far from the main highway. I must have been getting close to that highway, I realise now, when I saw the man in the yellow cap.

It caught the sunshine that slanted down through a gap in the oak leaves arching the track. It swayed to and fro, that bright spot of yellow, like a daffodil in a March wind. And it swayed because the man who wore it was struggling in the grasp of two others.

'Robin looks for trouble,' my mother used to complain. I do not know about that. When you see two great ragged fellows (outlaws by the look of them) setting upon a lonely traveller, and an old man at that, you can hardly walk off in the opposite direction.

I did the only thing I could. I ran forward, whipping out my knife. The clappers hung from my girdle, rattling against my thigh, but in the excitement of the moment I thought no more of them.

The old man was crying out in a language I did not understand. He was a Jew, of course. I had known that much from my first glimpse of his pointed yellow cap. There were plenty of those to be seen in Oxford, for all Jews had to wear them.

Suddenly he went down. One of his attackers turned away to catch the laden packhorse — there were two beasts, the packhorse and a riding horse, and they were both drifting away down the road. The second outlaw stooped over the old man and I saw the flash of steel.

I was still twenty yards away. I had hoped to take him by surprise, but I dared wait no longer, or the Jew's throat would be cut.

I let out a yell. The outlaw glanced round as I had

7

meant him to. He was a rugged-looking villain, not one I would have chosen to take on, especially as he had a friend to help him. But you cannot think these things out calmly at the time. Come to that, it was only an hour or two since I had been wishing myself dead, but I forgot all that as I bore down on the outlaw. My first concern just then was to stay alive.

I need not have worried. He took one look at me and uttered a yell far more blood-curdling than my own. If I had been a demon straight from Hell, coming at him with a red-hot pitchfork, he could not have put more stark terror into his cry.

He did not wait. He ran like a stag and went crashing away through the undergrowth. His friend turned, took in the situation, and bounded after him.

It may seem hard to believe now, but I did not grasp the reason for their panic. I had not yet got used to being a leper. Those outlaws were the very first strangers I had had to face in the special garb which marked me as unclean. I was surprised at their cowardice, but I had more urgent things to think about.

I dropped to my knees and cradled the old man's head on my lap. The yellow cap had fallen off to reveal a bald brown skull, with tufts of woolly grey curls above each ear. His beard too was grey and curling. His mouth had fallen open and there was a trickle of blood from a cut lip. I could see no serious wound.

He stirred. His eyelids fluttered. He groaned and muttered something in his own speech. Then he opened his eyes properly, dark and gentle eyes they were, and the fear died as he looked up into my face and saw that I was not one of his attackers.

'It's all right,' I said. 'They've gone. They'll not come back.'

'Thank you,' he said softly.

'Are you hurt?'

'No, no. I think not.' He spoke English awkwardly, giving the words a foreign sound. 'They were a little rough — at my age it is upsetting — but you came before they could do me any lasting injury.'

Then, rather late in the day, I remembered.

The blood rushed to my face. I was no longer holding him — he was sitting up, supported on one elbow. None the less, I scrambled to my feet and backed away.

'God forgive me, sir! I may have done you a worse injury than those men could. I never thought! I should not have touched you. I should have let you lie. You see how it is with me? I — I — '

I could not bring myself to speak the word and say what I was. Anyhow he could see for himself now, from my hooded cloak and the tell-tale clappers at my girdle.

If I had expected him to swoon again from sheer fright I was much mistaken.

He actually smiled.

'You are a leper?' he said in his gentle voice, more surprised and interested than panic-stricken.

'Yes. I lifted your head — I wanted to make sure you were alive. Everything else went out of my mind — '

'Naturally! Do not worry, my boy,' he said soothingly, 'I am not afraid. I have seen much of this disease. I do not believe it is as contagious as men say. I would sooner be helped by a leper than have my throat slit by the healthiest scoundrel in the kingdom.' He actually laughed and I could not help smiling in reply.

'Sherwood is a dangerous place, sir. What possessed you to travel by yourself?'

'Ah, but I am not alone.' He got to his feet, a little

shakily, and peered down the road. 'I have my servant — those fellows would not have ventured if he had been with me.'

'Then where . . . ?'

'Pierre had a notion we took the wrong fork of the road. Is this the way to Nottingham?'

'No, sir.'

'Then he was right. He turned back to make sure. But as I was tired he persuaded me to rest here — he's a good fellow, he only wanted to save me needless riding —'

'It was unwise, sir, all the same.'

I was wondering whether to offer to catch the horses before they strayed further, but I was still nervous of touching anything, even their bridles.

He stooped and picked up his yellow cap and carefully put it on. The Jews (I was to learn) dislike going with uncovered heads. Even in their own houses they wear at least a skull-cap, especially for study or prayer.

He looked at me with a curiously keen expression. Gentle his eyes might be, but they were penetrating. He said:

'How long have you been afflicted?'

'It has come upon me only in this last month. In fact —' I hesitated only a moment, for he was not a man from whom you could hide things, and in any case what was the point? 'I was declared unclean this very morning,' I concluded.

'So?' His eyebrows went up. 'Show me your hands, my boy. Turn them over. So.' He asked me a few questions. Any fever? Pains? Numbness? Any other rashes or marks on my skin beyond what he could see? I could tell he had difficulty in finding all the right words in English. I helped him out by answering in my scholar's Latin. Again his eyebrows went up in surprise but he made no comment. He went on with his questions, wagging his beard at my replies.

At last he paused. 'Good! Very good. My boy, there is one last thing I want to ask you.'

'Yes, sir?'

His dark eyes twinkled either side of his long hooked nose. 'What ignorant fool told you that you had leprosy?' he said.

CHAPTER THREE

'One Must Get Used to Risks'

BEFORE I went to Oxford, when I was a simple village boy, I should have been shocked if anyone had suggested that a priest could be an ignorant fool.

Now I just answered: 'It was our parson at Westwood.'

'Is he a doctor?'

'No, sir — but the priest has to decide these things.'

'Well, I meant no disrespect to your parson. I am sure he is a most worthy man. Many a doctor has been mistaken about this disease. But I am one with a fair experience and I will stake my reputation: you have nothing but a harmless skin affection. I have an ointment in my medicine-chest yonder. It will clear up your trouble in a week or two.'

I stared at him. 'You swear this?' I said huskily.

He smiled. 'What oath can I take that would convince a Christian? But why should I trick you with false hopes when you have saved my life?' He chuckled. 'I am not even trying to sell you the ointment. It will be free.'

This man was not lying. He looked so wise and gentle, he had the strength of knowledge and quiet certainty. I could not doubt him, and a wave of joy swept over me. I fell on my knees in the dust, thanking God and vowing candles to every Saint I had ever prayed to.

My hood must have fallen back, so that as he looked down on my bent head he must have noticed the shaven circle of my tonsure. As he raised me to my feet he inquired in a puzzled tone:

'You are not yourself a priest surely? At your age? Or a monk?'

I explained about Oxford, and how all the scholars had to begin as if they meant to take holy orders, though in the end a good number of them did not go on to make their full vows. There was no other way to acquire learning.

Again he chuckled. 'I see. And to gain learning it is worth sacrificing some of this brown thatch of yours! It soon grows again.'

I grinned, more myself again now. I knew that the short bristles were already sprouting from my bare crown. It did not matter in the village, but I should have to get my head newly shaven when I went back to Oxford in the autumn.

A new thought struck me and wiped the grin from my lips. *Should* I be going back to Oxford? Even if the Jew's ointment worked, might there not still be difficulties?

Perhaps he read my mind. 'Well, my boy, what do we do now?' He stepped across the green verge to the packhorse, which had moved back towards us, and I, to be helpful, went over and took the bridle of the other beast.

'Do, sir?' I said over my shoulder.

He was busy unfastening some straps. 'Yes. I can give you the ointment. I can bandage your hands. I can safely promise you a complete cure before the month is out. You believe me?'

'Yes!'

'But will this priest? Even if I go with you now myself and speak to him?' We both knew the answer to that question. I could see that the Jew thought the same as I did. And he had never met Father Simon.

'It is awkward,' I said. 'He has published his decision to

the whole parish. He is not a man who likes to be proved wrong.'

'Who does? Hold out your hands.' He began to dress them with the ointment. It was cool and soothing, with a subtle aroma that was rather pleasant. Deftly he criss-crossed my palms and wrists with linen bandages, leaving my fingers and thumbs free. 'Perhaps he will be more ready to admit his mistake in a few weeks' time, when all the symptoms have disappeared.'

'He should be,' I murmured.

'And meanwhile? That is the problem. You agree, you cannot go straight back to the village — they will drive you out again. You certainly must not go to the leper's hospital. You are not a leper — now. But you might well become one, living among real sufferers.'

'I'd sleep in the woods before I'd do that!'

'Even that may not be necessary. First, obviously, you must get rid of these alarming clothes. I can let you have Pierre's spare tunic and shoes out of the saddle-bag. Where can the man have got to?' He looked anxiously down the road. We had by now been talking a full half-hour.

'I hope he did not meet the fellows who attacked you,' I said.

He laughed aloud, his teeth gleaming through his beard. 'I doubt that — even if they were not already pal-sied with terror as you say! Wait till you see Pierre. He is a quick-tempered Gascon, and you know what they are. Pierre can look after himself — just as he looks after me. In these troubled times a Jew is wise to employ a Gentile bodyguard.'

Privately I thought that Pierre had not been of much use on this occasion. But even the best servant cannot be in two places at once, and it had all turned out most luckily for me.

I accepted the clothes which the Jew pulled out of the saddle-bag. He asked me my name and told me his own, Solomon of Stamford. He lived in Nottingham and was on his way there.

Thankfully I buried the tell-tale leper garb in a bed of rotting leaves and threw that wretched clapper as far as I could into the woodland.

I see now what a gesture of defiance it was, what an act of faith in my new acquaintance. I had been told I was unclean, solemnly proclaimed in church, publicly cast out, with a long list of 'do's' and 'don'ts'. All this I was ignoring. I was setting my own judgement against authority. Had I been older, and known more of the world, I wonder if I would have dared?

'That is better,' said Solomon with an approving wag of his head as I came out of the undergrowth. 'It will be less alarming for Pierre when he returns. We can tell him simply that your own clothes were very ragged and I wished to reward you. You are a poor scholar, travelling the roads — not an uncommon sight at this season.'

'And it is true — now.'

'Yes. But the question is, do you wish to travel the roads until your hands heal? If so, I will give you money — it would be a small return for your service. If not — ' and he eyed me with a keen, almost appealing gaze — 'would you come on to the city with us? You would be welcome in my home. What is more, I could keep an eye on the cure — alter the treatment if necessary. What do you say?'

What could I say but a grateful 'yes'?

I was like a boat adrift. In the space of a day or two my whole life had been changed and now changed a second time. There had been no calm period in which to consider where I was going. That very morning I had been cast forth from my own family with little hope of ever

seeing them again. The hope was much greater now —
after an interval — but in the meantime I was utterly
alone. No wonder I was ready to turn to Solomon of
Stamford, foreign though he was in birth and religion,
and accept him almost in place of the father I had left
behind.

Somehow I had to get through the next week or two,
and I should have been a fool to lose contact with the
doctor treating me. I had no notion then that my choice
would twist my life into an entirely new direction.

'Ah, my trusty bodyguard!' Solomon exclaimed, cutting short my thanks.

Pierre came up the road at a canter. He was a swarthy
black-haired Frenchman from the South, an ugly devil
with a broken nose. He was not a big man — I had
guessed that from my borrowed clothes and I myself was
not fully grown then — but I saw why the Jew had
spoken of him with respect. Pierre rode like a soldier. A
sword hung at his saddle-bow and a long dagger at his
belt. He looked as though he knew how to use them both.

He was taken aback to see me and (unless it was my

fancy) not best pleased. Perhaps he recognised his blue tunic on me and wondered what had been happening. Solomon told him quickly about the robbers and their panic at my approach. As he could not mention the real reason for it it made me sound more of a hero than I deserved.

Pierre swore and struck his palm with his fist, angry at missing it all.

'I am sorry, master! I thought you would be safe enough. I did not meet a soul myself until I reached the main road.'

'You were right, then?' said the doctor soothingly. 'We had taken the wrong fork?'

'Ay. You must come back to the last turning. Then it is a long mile to the Nottingham highway.'

'In that case let us be moving, if we are to make the city before dark. Robin is coming with us. You and he can take turns to walk and ride.'

'By all means,' said the Gascon with as good a grace as he could muster, and if he was not exactly delighted, who could blame him? Through no fault of his own he had been missing when he was most wanted, and now he was being told to share his horse with an unknown youth who had already done his job for him and was wearing his spare shoes and tunic. I should have been surly myself.

I thanked him in my scholar's French and made a private resolution that I would not mount his horse unless I was positively ordered to. If I was to spend a week or two in this household it might be better not to earn Pierre's ill will.

My heart was so light, I think I could have danced those miles to Nottingham, never mind walked. The doom had been lifted from me. I lived again. The very colours of the summer day seemed brighter than before

—the dappled black and silver of the birch trunks, the sheen of the bracken, the blue dazzle of the sky between the nodding boughs. I began to sing as I marched at the doctor's stirrup. I stopped with an apology but he bent down and told me to go on. So, as the sun westered, we climbed the last low ridge dividing us from our destination.

'Listen, Robin—'

'Yes, sir?'

'While you lodge with us I must ask you to behave with—with some discretion.'

'Of course, sir.' But I was not clear what he meant.

'Things are not easy for us Jews. We have many enemies and we have to walk carefully. We have been accused of terrible things—fantastic things. Need I say, falsely?'

I murmured politely. I knew what he meant. I had heard wild stories—of Christian children kidnapped and murdered or forced into becoming Jews, of strange unholy rites and dreadful sacrilege against the Church. I did not know whether such tales were true or false, but I could not believe them of Solomon.

'If people see your shaven crown,' he said, 'they may accuse me of harbouring runaway monks or some such nonsense.' I laughed. 'It will be best if you stay in the house and show yourself as little as possible, at least to begin with.'

'As you wish, sir. But if you are treating me, doesn't that explain why I am there?'

A shadow crossed his face. 'You must not say that I am treating you.'

'But—'

'I am breaking the law by doing so. Since last year it has been forbidden for Jewish doctors to practise in England.'

I had not known that. I said: 'You are taking a risk for me, then?'

'One must get used to risks — especially if one is a Jew. Do not worry, Robin. Many of us still practise and the Christians turn a blind eye to the law. A good doctor is a good doctor, and when a man is sick he cares only about getting well. But some things are not to be shouted from the housetops.'

'I understand, sir.'

I had no wish to shout anything from the housetops. I had my own secret to keep.

Sunset was near as we came out of the forest fringe, over the sandy crest, and looked down upon the city, huddled within its wall and ditch. It is an up-and-down place, not flat like Oxford, but with about as many people, I suppose: two or three thousand. In those days I had seen nowhere larger.

The royal castle crouched at one end like a lion upon its tawny rock. Behind and above the thatched house-tops, glittering golden through the veil of wood-smoke from a hundred kitchens, the Trent unwound its snaky coils.

Solomon nodded towards a lonely group of buildings which we were passing. 'St Leonard's leper-house,' he murmured. 'The inmates are entitled to the meat of any deer found dead in the forest.' I wrinkled up my nose and thanked Heaven that I should not need to depend on such charities.

We had seen few travellers on the road but now we mingled with townsmen driving in their cattle and sheep for the night. We went through the gate with them un-challenged. The watchman greeted Solomon by name. We continued in single file beneath the overhanging gables of Cow Lane. This time I wrinkled up my nose because of the stench from so many yards and dwellings, so closely packed. I had passed through Nottingham before only in autumn and early summer, and known Oxford in the cool months between. I had not dreamt how foul a city could become by August. I was glad when we came out by the Butter Cross and breathed the air of the vast market-place.

Nottingham is really two towns, the old English quarter and the French part which grew up later in the shelter of the castle. At the time I am speaking of (It was in the first King Edward's time, in the year 1290) the Jews still had their own district or ghetto, a miniature town within a town. It lay at one corner of the French quarter, between the streets called Hounds Gate and Castle Gate. Their houses stood shoulder to shoulder, like men always ready for attack. Blank walls, or only the tiniest windows, high up, looked outwards at the world. There was one gate and one gate only, heavily studded and barred.

Through that gate I walked at Solomon's stirrup, and found myself in a small courtyard, already shadowy with twilight. Black-haired women were gossiping as they drew water from a well in the middle. Solomon urged his horse on, down a narrow alley, and into a second courtyard. All the houses faced inwards on to these courts. The windows here were bigger, they glimmered with soft golden light, and there was a fine blend of cooking smells from half a dozen kitchens.

I helped the doctor as he slid from the saddle. Pierre led both horses away. Solomon took me up some stone steps and through an arched doorway.

'Welcome to my home,' he said, turning with a smile.

Before I could make any suitable reply there was an excited babble of Hebrew overhead and someone came rustling down the spiral staircase. Solomon laughed and called out and started across the room, arms outspread, the long sleeves of his gown like wings.

'Susanna!'

The candlelight glimmered on bright black hair and eager eyes. Then, for some moments, the girl vanished in the folds of his embrace. I stood there, while he answered her muffled questions and exclamations in a soothing amused tone.

Suddenly I saw her face again, peeping at me round Solomon's shoulder, dark liquid eyes wide open like a nervous deer's. Solomon relaxed his hold and swung round to me again.

'We must talk English now, my daughter. We have a guest. This is Robin of Westwood.'

'A Gentile!'

Her face clouded. She sounded hostile. I bowed and smiled but got no smile in answer.

I do not think Solomon could ever be very stern with his daughter, but he spoke to her as severely as he could.

'Remember, Susanna, what it says in the Torah.' And he went on to quote something which struck an echo in my mind, and puzzled me until I realised that I had read it myself in Latin in our own Bible, in Leviticus. ' "The stranger that dwelleth with you shall be unto you as one born among you, and thou shalt love him as thyself. For ye too were strangers in the land of Egypt." '

Susanna bent her head meekly and offered me her plump little hand, then drew it back as she saw my bandages.

'You are welcome to my father's house,' she said.

But as I bowed again I did not feel it likely that she would ever love *me* as much as she loved herself.

CHAPTER FOUR

A Stranger in the Ghetto

'A N D now, here is my son David — '

I found myself being warmly, in fact emotionally, greeted by a youth perhaps my elder by a couple of years.

'I want to thank you! You saved my father's life!'

If David ben Solomon had been a girl you would have called him beautiful. He was very like his sister in feature, finely moulded and sensitive, but the resemblance ended there. David was hard and lean, with nothing else girlish about him, and *his* eyes did not make me think of a nervous deer's. They were more like black fires, if you can imagine such a thing.

I cannot remember what I stammered out in answer. Solomon came to my rescue with a jovial cry. 'Supper, children! That is the best way to thank our guest — and to save your poor old father's life a second time. For my part, I am famished, and Robin must be too.'

An old maid-servant brought warm water, fragrantly perfumed, and linen towels, and I dipped my fingers in as best I could. I had heard strange things about the Jews and their customs and I was a little surprised to find myself bidden to their family table. But the feelings of strangeness did not last long. They said their own grace, I crossed myself and murmured my college Latin, and then we started one of the best meals I had ever tasted. The meat was excellent beef, we drank strong red wine instead of ale, and there were raisins, figs and marzipan sweetmeats that to me had been so far undreamt-of luxuries.

It had been a long day, I had been through a great deal, and the wine, as I say, was strong. I grew drowsy and found it an effort to concentrate on the conversation. They spoke so fast, so quick-wittedly, and their alien accent made them hard to follow, and sometimes they dropped into their own speech. It is not surprising that I have only vague memories of that evening. Somehow I dragged myself up the winding stairs behind David. There was a soft mattress in a curtained alcove, a pillow smelling of lavender, cool crisp linen against my flesh, such comfort as I had never known. As my head went down, so I too went down, deep into a pool of oblivion. I did not wake till the sun was high. David was beside me, laying out clean clothes of his own for me to try on.

For two weeks I did not stray outside the ghetto. Indeed, beyond taking the air in the courtyard for a little while, I never set foot outside the doctor's house. Every morning he looked at my sores and assured me that they were healing. Susanna usually put on the fresh bandages.

She was my chief companion until the evening. Her father was often out or shut up with his books and medicines. David too was absent a good deal: I did not know what he was doing and dared not ask. I sensed that this family, however friendly, had learnt to guard its secrets. But the girl never went into the town alone, so, apart from running into the other houses of the ghetto or pausing for a gossip in the courtyard, much of her time was spent in spinning or embroidery. The old woman, Miriam, did most of the housework.

I seemed to fascinate Susanna, as though I were some strange creature trapped and brought into the home as a pet—or perhaps just a curiosity. Once I said so. She opened her eyes wide.

'But of course, Robin! Don't you realise? I have never talked to a Gentile. It is different for Father and David —they go out into the world.'

'What about Pierre?'

She screwed up her face. 'Pooh!'

'Pierre is a Gentile.'

'I could not talk to him. I should not wish to. It suits my father to employ him. It suits Pierre to work for him —but only, I suspect, because he cannot find a Christian master.' That was my own private suspicion, though I said nothing. I had never much fancied the Gascon. He looked to me like a man with an ugly past. But a tough bodyguard was necessary for an elderly man travelling, and a Jew could not be too particular.

Susanna would ask me the simplest questions about ordinary life outside and about my studies at Oxford— at least, not so much my studies (for she had no interest in learning) as how we young scholars went on there. She went into fits of laughter when she heard of the tricks we played on each other and the townsmen and—when we dared—on the solemn old men who lectured to us.

She was intrigued by my tonsure, now fast vanishing under a growth of new hair.

'But you are not a priest! Or going to be one?'

'No. But even if we are not, so long as we are studying in the University we must have our heads shaved, keep a vow of celibacy—'

'What is that?'

'Celibacy? We must promise not to marry.'

'What an odd word! And what an odd idea! Our people have nothing like that.' She overcame her giggles. 'But if you do not become a priest, what will you do?'

25

'I'm not sure.' I hesitated. 'I have sometimes thought of becoming a physician like your father — but that means many more years of study, six or eight years perhaps. One cannot start Medicine until one is a Master of Arts.'

'It is too long, Robin. Especially with that dismal vow of — of — '

'Celibacy?'

'Yes. What can you do that is quicker?'

'Oh, there is always work for clerks.' I was a little vague myself. When the chance had come to escape from farm work I had seized it without hesitation. Once I could master reading and writing, once I could understand French, Latin and simple accounts, some lord or merchant would be glad to employ me. I had not yet got down to practical plans. I had several years to wait.

'I think,' said Susanna, 'you will go a little further than that.'

'Why do you think so?'

She answered quietly: 'I read it in your eyes. They will look higher than an ink pot.'

Her tone embarrassed me and I changed the subject.

Luckily there were always questions I could safely ask her — on the countless rules and customs of the household that puzzled me. Why could she cook beef but not suet? Why could we not have milk or anything made from milk at the same meal as meat, and why must even the cooking-vessels be kept separate? Why could not linen and wool be mixed in the same piece of clothing?

'It is the Law,' she would say, 'but if you want chapter and verse you had better ask my father.' I ought at least to accept the Torah, she argued, because it was what the Christians called the Old Testament. Of course, the Torah needed a lot of explaining, so learned rabbis had written the Talmud. What wasn't in one book must be in the other.

At Oxford they had taught us that the Bible needed a heap of books to explain it, written by the early fathers of the Church and other devout men. Now I realised that the Jews, who shared the Old Testament with us, had scholars to interpret it in their own fashion.

Susanna, however, had not my love of abstract argument. She accepted the Law as laid down by her father and by the rabbi in the tiny synagogue overlooking Lister Gate. The important thing to do with the Holy Scriptures, she seemed to feel, was to make sure that the right texts were written on scraps of parchment and put into little boxes as amulets or lucky charms. One such box, a *mezuza*, was fixed to the doorpost as a sign that this was a Jewish home. Two others, made of black leather, the *tephilin* or phylacteries, were strapped on forehead and left arm at morning prayers.

'They keep away demons,' said Susanna.

'They are to remind us of the Law,' her father corrected her mildly.

Being a girl, Susanna did not wear these amulets. David teased her and said that no demon would dare to come within miles of her anyhow. Myself, I thought it a curious way to use the Scriptures, but it would not have been polite to say so. I knew what David would have retorted: was it more curious than our Christian way of encasing a hair or tooth from some long dead Saint, or even a splinter or a rusty nail? Those days in the Nottingham ghetto taught me, faster than months in the Oxford schools, that there were more ways than one of looking at things.

I liked to get Solomon talking in the evening, for he

knew the world and his mind was stored with experience. It was an open mind, too. No argument shocked him. No subject was banned.

'No part of human knowledge lies outside the Jewish way,' he used to insist. 'That was the teaching of Moses ben Maimon, whom many of us call the Light of Israel.'

'Who was he?' I had to ask.

'A rabbi, but also a physician like myself. He simplified and explained the Law for us, so that we could follow it in the world of our own times. He lived in Spain, at Cordova, a hundred years ago.'

'Father was born in Spain,' said Susanna.

He nodded. 'I should properly call myself Solomon of Seville. But I was taken to Stamford when I was a youth, and —' he hesitated and smiled slyly — 'in England it is wiser to look as though you belong!'

David snorted. 'A Jew can never belong! They will not let us.'

'It is better in Spain, though,' said his sister. 'Father should take us there.'

'We shall see, my child.'

There was silence. I knew what was in all their minds.

Long ago the Jews had been welcomed in England, especially by kings who wanted to borrow money. Gradually, over the years, they had become more and more unpopular with the people, less and less necessary to the kings, who found that they could get loans elsewhere. Bit by bit the Jews had been restricted. First, they were limited to living in twenty-five permitted towns: nowhere else. Later they were debarred from holding land; later still, from lending money at interest; finally, last year, from practising as doctors. I had a shrewd suspicion that the money-lending, like the doctoring, continued unofficially.

'But of course!' exclaimed David when I once hinted at this. 'How else can most of our people exist?'

I said mildly that money-lenders were nearly always unpopular. It was unfortunate that so many of his brethren sought their living that way.

'Tell me some other ways!' he thundered.

I was taken aback. I began to stammer and rack my brains, but he did not wait for my answer.

'Think, Robin!' His voice had dropped, but he was still furious. 'Can I take up a trade—or learn a craft? Not unless I am apprenticed to a member of some guild. And do not all your guilds make their members take Christian oaths? How then can I—a Jew—become a blacksmith or a tailor or a grocer or anything else?'

I saw his point. He went on.

'Can I enter your university? You know I cannot. So I cannot become a lawyer or any sort of clerk. I might have the wisest brain in the world, yet all your learning is barred to me. Or I might have the heart of a lion—yet I cannot go to the wars with the King! No Jew can be a knight—again it is a question of vows, vows, vows, always your Christian vows! So I cannot fight, I cannot hold land, I cannot work with my hands, I cannot do business or study or teach—since last year I could not even heal the sick, like my father, if I had the skill and the wish to do so, which I have not! And then you ask why so many of my people have to be money-lenders. How much choice have *your* people given us? Even that is nowadays illegal. Can you blame us if we evade the law, so long as there are Christians begging us to do so?' He gave a bitter laugh. 'Do you know how many of your churches were built with Jewish loans? I could name you half a dozen Cistercian abbeys alone. Aaron of Lincoln used to boast that he, more than any other man, had built St Albans.'

I could think of no reasonable answer to his eloquence. And after all these years I have not thought of one yet.

The storm over as suddenly as it had blown up, David grinned and patted my shoulder. 'Forgive me. Like some of my father's mixtures, I come quickly to boiling-point. But remember, Robin: my people may be as God made them, but they are as you Gentiles have made them too!'

I could sympathise. Most of us, I know, have to accept the lot we are born with. Of a hundred peasant boys, ninety-nine will never get away from the plough. They might be Jews or Saracens for all the hope they have of rising to be knights and gentlemen. But at least for one in a hundred, like myself, there is some chance to break away, some choice among the humbler trades and livelihoods. For all the chains that bind us we are not complete captives of circumstance, like the Jews when they live in a Christian kingdom.

Do not suppose that those weeks in Solomon's house were continually overshadowed by such talk. Whatever the family had on their minds, the general atmosphere was sunny, often gay. I look back on those days as serene and happy, as I watched the daily improvement of my skin and knew beyond doubt that Solomon's diagnosis had been correct. Without any disloyalty to my own faith I slipped contentedly into the different ways of the household. I even came to look forward to the start of their Sabbath, when the sun went down behind the castle towers on a Friday evening and the special Sabbath meal was set out in the light of the seven-branched candlestick — the stuffed fish (which as a good Christian I could enjoy on a fast day, though I had to decline the meat), the delicious twisty loaves which Susanna baked, the smooth red wine flashing from the little goblets.

I can remember only one unpleasant day during that time. It was when I woke up early with a raging toothache.

It may seem a small matter to complain of, when I had been so recently freed from the fear of leprosy. But toothache is toothache. When you have it, you are in no state of mind to count your other blessings.

I mention it now because of the curious thing that happened.

Susanna noticed my strained look that morning and demanded the reason. 'There's only one way with a bad tooth,' she said cheerfully. 'Have it out.'

That was all very well for her. It was not her tooth.

'They say you can cure toothache by pricking a wood-louse with a needle, and then touching the tooth with the point.'

' "They say"!' she echoed mockingly. 'Have you ever known it work?'

'I have not, myself.'

'If you believe in that treatment, Robin, I will lend you my needle. The wood-louse you must find for yourself. But I am sure you would do better to have the tooth out.'

I had a private fear that the girl was right. But braver men than I are cowards when it comes to tooth-drawing. I have seen it done by the village blacksmith, I have seen it done by wandering quacks in the market place, and, though they all boast that there is nothing to it, the patient — to judge from his shouts and struggles — usually takes a different view.

'It may pass off,' I said feebly.

'You are not afraid of the pain, Robin?'

I hesitated. Meeting her eyes, I could only grin in a twisted way and say, 'Yes. I am.'

'My father could draw your tooth and you would feel nothing.'

'Then he works greater miracles than most of the Saints!' I retorted.

'It is true, though. Robin, why not let him see, at least? Perhaps,' she added cunningly, 'he will say that there is no need to lose it. He has a wonderful spiced oil. Sometimes one drop will take away the ache. It is much better than a needle and a wood-louse.'

She was good at persuading. That afternoon I was taken into Solomon's room for the first time. I glanced round me with a somewhat fearful curiosity, taking in the books and bottles and boxes, the mortar and pestle for crushing powders, the leaden slab for compounding ointments, and the bags of drying herbs. On any other occasion I would have been begging him to explain everything. Now my eyes were rolling like a frightened horse's, questing for the dreadful instruments I felt certain must be there. A gentle hand on my shoulder pressed me down on to a stool facing the window.

'Open your mouth. So.' I blinked in the sunshine. He loomed over me darkly, peering into my jaws. 'On the left, at the back? So. I have no doubt it aches!'

'There must be a worm in it,' I said.

'Perhaps. I have never seen this worm that makes teeth rot like apples — that does not mean it does not exist, but it must be very small. Rotten your tooth certainly is, and no more use to you.'

My heart sank. If Solomon offered to pull it out, how could I refuse? I wished he were younger and stronger, but I could scarcely tell him that I would prefer to go to a barber or a blacksmith. I should just have to be brave.

I did not, of course, believe the story that he could draw the tooth without hurting me. Every fair-ground quack made that promise.

'I expect,' said Solomon kindly, 'you only wish that you could go to sleep tonight and wake up tomorrow with the pain gone — and the tooth with it?'

'That would be wonderful,' I agreed.

'Or even this afternoon?'

'Better still, sir — if only it were possible!'

'So.' His voice was even gentler than usual. It was like a caressing hand. 'You were awake very early. I think you are sleepy now?' I yawned. 'Have you ever noticed this gold ring I wear?' He held up his hand. The ring caught the sunbeam slanting dustily through the narrow window. 'Look at it closely. It is a very rare and remarkable ring.' I could not see that it was, but then, I was finding it increasingly hard to keep my eyes open. Nor did he keep his hand still for two moments together — he moved it in slow, rhythmic sweeps before my face. 'You are getting very sleepy,' he purred, *very* sleepy.' The ring winked back at me. 'I am going to count. When I reach ten you will be fast asleep. One, two, three, four . . .'

There was a taste of salt on my lips.

'Here,' said Solomon, 'spit into this.'

I opened my eyes and saw the basin he held. I saw the red blood in it when I spat. 'Here is your tooth, Robin,' he said, displaying it between finger and thumb. 'If you can see a worm at the root you have sharper eyes than I.'

'But — but — ' I stammered. 'I felt nothing — I — '

'You were asleep.'

'This is magic!' I was alarmed and relieved at the same time. 'You put a spell on me!'

He wagged his head. 'I know no spells. You wished to go to sleep, so I was able to help you a little. If you had not been willing — if you had been determined to stay awake — I could have done nothing.'

'It is very wonderful, none the less.' I bent over the basin again. There was less blood now. My mouth was sore but the toothache had gone. 'If you did this in the market place,' I said, 'you would soon be a rich man.'

He smiled sadly. 'How innocent you are, my dear boy! If I used this method in the market place I should be burnt to death as a sorcerer.'

I saw what he meant, but I was thankful that he had trusted in me enough to cure my pain. As he had said before, a Jew got used to taking risks.

CHAPTER FIVE

The Coming of the King

THREE days later I was holding out my hands and studying them with delight. I had never seen them so pale and smooth, with neither a blister from farm work nor an ink stain from study. I was cured.

'So.' Solomon gave a little grunt of approval. 'You can put away your bandages, Susanna. Robin needs no more treatment. It is better now for the fresh air and light to reach his skin.'

'Thank you again,' I said huskily.

'And now you will be leaving us?' said Susanna. It may have been politeness, but I think she sounded sorry.

'Yes,' I said. 'The scholars go back to Oxford in October. But I cannot show my face there until I have seen Father Simon. He must verify my cure and give me a letter to the Warden.'

I felt strangely reluctant to leave this quiet home. I liked them all so much and they had opened my eyes to so much I had not known before. I was eager, though, to see my family and set their minds at rest. I should be like Lazarus indeed, brought back from the dead.

'You must ride my horse,' Solomon insisted. 'David will be glad to ride with you, and he can take Pierre —'

'I will go, too,' interrupted Susanna. 'I have never ridden into Sherwood. But not tomorrow. The day after.'

'As you please,' I said, 'and thank you. But why not tomorrow?'

'Because of something my friend Sarah told me just now at the well.'

'More gossip?' said Solomon.

'Not gossip, Father. It is all over the town. The King's Marshal arrived last night. His officers are chalking all the doors of the houses for billets.'

'So? The King is coming to Nottingham?'

'And the Queen. Tomorrow. I would not like to miss that.'

'Nor would I,' I said. 'The next day will be time enough to go home.'

The ghetto was not, of course, affected by the billeting arrangements, though I fancy that the Jewish families had to collect a purse of money for the King's entertainment in the Castle. And the next afternoon, when word came that the royal column had been sighted, straggling across Trent Bridge and along the causeway over the water-meadows to the town gate, the Jews streamed out in their yellow caps to watch the arrival. Susanna and the other women came too.

We took our stand on the corner of Friar Lane and the market place, just below the Carmelite convent, a good place because the procession had to come slowly up the hill towards us and then turn left for the last long pull up to the Castle Rock.

We had a fine view of the King. The first Edward, that was, Edward of Westminster, better known by his nickname 'Longshanks'. I could see why, for even on horseback he showed his tallness, with his great legs dangling straight on either side of the Spanish jennet he rode.

He was just over fifty then. His beard had lost the early red-gold brightness of the Plantagenets and had darkened. There was good humour in the face that turned to smile into the crowd. There was a terrible strength also — I could imagine that face, grim and steel-hard inside a helmet, surveying the rebel barons at Evesham long ago, or the Welsh raiders, or the Saracens during his Crusade. A great man, Edward the First, and how different from his son!

He passed by, with his Chancellor and his chaplain and a string of notables, lords and knights and officers of the royal household, and the Mayor of Nottingham and the sheriffs of the two halves of the town, enjoying their brief hour of glory as they escorted their King to his own castle gateway.

'Empty-headed dolts!' David hissed in my ear.

I saw that he was glaring not at the Mayor and his companions in their long furred gowns but at the courtiers. I could see nothing much wrong with them myself, apart from the way they looked — or did not even trouble to look — at the people doffing their caps and curtseying as they went by. Some of them were certainly rather supercilious. Others behaved as though the common folk did not exist. The King, I could believe, was of quite another type. He would mix with all classes and, when food ran short on campaign, share his last wine with his men. He was as happy in homespun as in his royal robes, he would make a joke with anybody, and he was not afraid to get his own hands dirty if there was urgent work to be done.

The men riding behind him were more conscious of their own dignity. Some had sharp hawklike features, others were red-faced and puffy with good living.

'Our rulers,' David went on in a vicious undertone. 'And what do they understand, what do they know, beyond hunting and war?'

I read a sort of envy in his words. It was not simply that David despised these noblemen because their minds were limited. He too would have loved to ride out on a splendid horse, falcon on wrist, and share in the sports that they did. I think he would have gone to battle, too, in a good cause. From all this he was shut out by his Jewish faith.

Susanna felt much the same, in her girl's fashion. She adored rich gems and luxurious furs and materials, velvet and Cyprus brocade, sarsenet and cloth of gold. She was born to flounce about some castle hall to the strains of music from the minstrel gallery, not to live like a mouse in the ghetto.

I saw the yearning in her eyes as the royal carriages brought the Queen and her ladies up Wheeler Gate. Magnificent, clumsy contrivances they were, hooped over against the weather, fluttering with silk curtains. Each was drawn by several gaudily caparisoned horses in single file, straining against the gradient and the awkward right-angle turn. We got a good look at the Queen as her carriage trundled by.

'Eleanor of Castile,' said Solomon wistfully, as if her name stirred memories of his early days in Spain. 'She is still beautiful.'

I was glad to have seen her. She was said to be, in her own way, as remarkable as her husband. She had been with him to the Crusade and had saved his life, so went the story, by sucking poison from his wound. He had been fifteen when he married her and at fifty he was still deeply in love with her. That fact spoke volumes for her charm. Even in those days I had learnt that kings seldom made the most devoted of husbands.

The last carriage creaked up Friar Lane. Now there were only the waggons with stores and equipment. The crowd shredded away.

'So,' murmured Susanna with a sigh, half of contentment, half of vague unrest, 'I have seen the Queen.'

38

'I too,' said I. 'But I would have liked to see her longer. I doubt if I shall ever see her again.'

'Perhaps none of us will,' said Solomon in an odd voice.

He would not explain himself when Susanna pressed him. I turned his words over in my mind, trying possible interpretations. Had his doctor's eyes seen the mark of some mortal sickness in that face which to me had looked, though smiling, rather tired and drawn? If so, no wonder he would not say more. It was treason to foretell the death of royalty.

Solomon continued gloomy throughout that last day, and, as I have said, my own feelings were mixed as my departure grew near.

We started the next day as soon as the family had held their morning prayers. Solomon was still wearing the leather *tephilin* and the fringed shawl he put on for these thrice-daily ceremonials. He was also wearing a very enigmatic expression as he offered me a blessing in his own language and added in English:

'Go with God, Robin, and prosper. Perhaps we shall meet again soon, perhaps never. It is as God wills, and remember that your God is mine also.'

I shook his hand and thanked him once more. Then I led the horse through the low arch of the ghetto and mounted in the street. The others were waiting, impatient to go. It was a golden September morning and the forest beckoned. There was only one small flaw to mar our enjoyment: Solomon insisted on Pierre going with us, so that David and his sister should not come back alone. But the tough-looking Gascon rode silently behind and did not intrude into our conversation.

That return journey to Westwood passed quickly. We went of course by the direct route, our horses were fresh, and my two friends revelled in the rare chance of a canter along the soft sandy roads between the oaks and bracken. All too soon I began to recognise familiar landmarks within a mile or two of my village.

When the trees thinned and the cleared land stretched before us, green common and blond stubble, to the distant cottages clustered round the church, David reined in his mare and said:

'Better we say good-bye here. My father said so. It will do you no good to have been staying with us.'

I knew what he meant, and I was sad because of it, and because of other things also. I slid from the saddle, gave the reins to Pierre and thanked him. Then I walked back to David and Susanna.

'We shall stay here and watch, until you are safely home,' David promised, 'but we won't show ourselves.'

I left them, sitting their horses motionless, in the dappled shadows on the forest edge. I could see figures gleaning in the cornfield. I squared my shoulders and strode forward into the sunlight.

Every head went up. Strangers are rare at Westwood. Many a day goes by without sight of a fresh face. Men and women alike, they all paused in their work, straightened up, and stood like a herd of deer surprised at grazing.

It was some time before anyone recognised me in the fine tunic and hose that were a parting gift from David. Then a man shouted, his voice high-pitched in alarm.

' 'Tes Robin come back! Hi, Robin — keep away, lad, ye've no right — '

I lifted my face to the sunshine. I laughed with joy. I began to run, my arms spread, showing my hands.

'I'm cured!' I sent my voice ringing across the great field. 'I'm not unclean! I never was!'

But they backed away, still doubtful. Only one figure

40

came towards me. It was my mother, gathering up her skirts as she hurried across the prickly stubble and the lumpy furrows of the strips already ploughed. Her face was working with emotion.

'Robin! Is it really true?'

'See for yourself, Mother!'

'Glory to God!' she cried chokingly as she saw my clear skin. Three more strides and our arms were round each other.

That bliss did not last long. I felt my arms gripped and twisted. We were wrenched apart. I was flung sprawling across the new-turned furrows. As I scrambled to my feet again my mother was being dragged away to a safe distance. Several men were glaring at me, fists clenched, sticks raised. Neighbours they were, men I had known since I was a child, but they menaced me like enemies.

'Have you gone crazed, Robin? Don't you come no nearer!'

'But I tell you, I'm all right —'

'I reckon that's for others to say.'

''Tes for Parson,' said another man.

'But look for yourselves! Look at my hands! There's naught wrong with them now.'

'Maybe — and maybe not. 'Tes not for us to judge of that.'

Nothing maddens me more than the stupidity of people who will not see what is under their noses. I do not know how long we should have stood there arguing. Luckily Father Simon was there walking among the gleaners and he came hurrying over the field as fast as his dignity allowed. My mother cried out to him, but her appeal was lost in the general hubbub as more and more villagers came on the scene.

Once more I held out my hands for all to see.

'I am cured, Your Reverence — '

There was an even louder howl from them all. A voice pealed above it scornfully: 'Who was ever cured of leprosy?' Again there was that howl. A crowd of frightened people can be more blood-curdling than a wolf pack.

When I could make myself heard I shouted: 'I never *had* leprosy! That was all a mistake!'

It was just as bad a mistake, on my own part, to say so in front of the whole village. Father Simon flushed. He took a step closer and peered at my hands. May he be forgiven for what he did that day, if he did it because he was too vain and ignorant to admit himself wrong! Perhaps it was only his eyes, which I know were weak.

'The disease is deceptive,' he announced importantly. 'It is easy for the sufferer to imagine that there is an improvement. I see no cause to alter my decision. Robert,' he went on severely, 'you are much at fault, coming back like this. You have defied the law. You risk grievous penalties — be thankful that we are your own folk and do not wish to add to your afflictions. Go now, keep the rules I gave you, let us have no more of this — '

'Yes, go!' They took up the cry. *'Go!'* It was a terrible chorus. More than ever they reminded me of wolves. They waved their sticks. Some of the men stooped for clods to throw.

'Wait! Cannot you behave like reasoning men instead of animals?'

It was David's voice, vibrant with fury. He came thundering across the common pasture like some knight in battle. There was a brief hush of astonishment, then a murmur as he drew rein beside me and they noted his yellow cap.

'Sir — ' David addressed himself to Father Simon as

politely as his excitement allowed. 'If you are still in doubt, may I assure you that Robin has been treated by one of the most skilled physicians in the kingdom?'

'Who?' demanded Father Simon, wavering.

'My own father, Solomon of Stamford, who as you may know —'

David was not allowed to finish. They all yelled and screamed.

'A Jew!'

'Jews aren't allowed to do doctoring!'

'Never heard of a Jew curing leprosy!'

'They cause it, more like! They poison the wells!'

I still feel sick when I recall that scene. There is no answer to blind hate and prejudice. Clods and stones began to rain on both of us. David's mare reared up, whinnying with alarm. Pierre galloped forward, swinging his sword and bellowing hideous oaths. Susanna was screaming from the forest, imploring us to come back.

We went. There was nothing else we could do. And, as there was nothing else they wanted, nobody pursued us. I scrambled back into the saddle, boiling with rage. There was one good thing: Mother knew that I was safe and well, and no one would be able to convince her that I was not.

We started back for Nottingham. I thanked David. He had taken a risk, I knew, interfering like that.

'I did more harm than good,' he said bitterly.

'Oh, no —'

'Yes! You can't reason with such people. There's only one thing that would have convinced them you were all right.'

'What?'

'We should have fitted you out with some pilgrim's badge,' said David cynically. 'I could have got you one

44

— you can buy anything if you know where to ask. You'd have sworn that you'd been to the holy shrine it came from. Preferably a shrine a long way off, so that there'd be no awkward questions.'

I was shocked. 'You mean — I'd have to lie? To pretend I'd made a pilgrimage when I hadn't? And been cured by a miracle?'

'It would have balanced things out. Those people won't believe what they see with their own eyes. And they won't accept the opinion of a man who knows. But they *would* believe in a miracle, because they want to!' David shrugged his shoulders. 'Of course, I can't expect you to see it as I do.'

I said nothing. His suggestion was wicked — I felt it must be — but I could not honestly say that it would not have worked.

Susanna changed the subject tactfully. 'Well,' she said, 'Father certainly did not expect that he would see Robin again as soon as this!'

I wondered. It occurred to me that Solomon might have had his misgivings all along. It could have accounted for his gloom. He had lived through so much in his time.

It was a thousand pities I had needed to go back to Westwood. But it was useless to present myself in Oxford without a clean bill of health, and I did not know how that was to be gained unless Father Simon could be persuaded.

Susanna leant over and pressed my hand. 'Cheer up, Robin! There is a home for you with us in Nottingham as long as you need it.'

But there, as I learnt before the day was over, the girl was sadly mistaken. When we reached the ghetto Solomon had news which quite overshadowed our own little adventure, and explained at last the anxious mood of the last day or two.

'The King has dealt us the final blow, my children.'

They stared in alarm. David said, 'What do you mean, Father?'

'I have had my forebodings. Now they have been confirmed officially — I have it from a royal servant. The King decrees that all Jews must quit England by All Saints' Day. We have less than two months and then we must be gone — forever.'

CHAPTER SIX

'No Word of This'

No time now to worry about my own future. The ghetto rang with lamentations.

Unlike Jews in other towns, the little group in Nottingham had led a quiet existence. No riots, no murders, had disturbed their peace. No horrors like the mass executions in London twelve years before, which had cost nearly three hundred Jewish lives.

In Nottingham only one or two far-sighted men like Solomon were even half prepared for the shock of the royal decree.

The Sheriff now published its terms. Every Jew must be out of England by the first of November. He might take such possessions as he could carry. Houses were forfeit to the King. Money on loan to Christians would be collected, free of interest, and paid into the King's Exchequer.

'In two words,' said David chokingly, 'exile and robbery!'

Where Jews lacked means to leave the country the King would pay their passages to Flanders.

'Take us further!' Susanna begged. 'Why not Seville? I have always dreamed of Spain.'

'I am considering all possibilities.' For the moment Solomon would say no more.

Susanna saw this news as a blessing in disguise. Watching her face, I could guess what she was thinking. Her sloe-dark eyes were bent on her needlework but in her mind she already beheld the golden city where her father had been born — the broad river, the plumed palm trees, the heady orange blossom, the bright fruit hung like a thousand little suns amid the greenery, the intense sunshine, the languorous heat. If this move meant Spain, I told myself, Susanna will not be sorry.

Her brother's reaction was quite different.

He flung about the house like a caged lion. I think he would have liked to barricade the ghetto and defend it like a fortress. He was a lost warrior, pining to fight under a banner that did not exist, a banner with the Star of another David for its device.

'You tell me to be patient, Father!' he groaned. 'We are men, remember, as well as Jews.'

The next afternoon Solomon beckoned me mysteriously into his room and closed the door.

'Robin, I must talk to you. David I cannot talk to — not in his present mood. But first promise me absolute secrecy.'

'I promise, sir.'

I felt rather embarrassed. What would David feel if he found out that his father had shared secrets with me instead of his own son?

'I have had a message, Robin. It is puzzling. And — considering the peril all Jews stand in at this moment — I find it rather disturbing.'

I could tell that from his grave manner. 'Yes, sir?' I said, and waited.

'The message amounts to a summons. I am bidden to leave the ghetto just before the gate is closed at dusk. The messenger will be waiting near by to conduct me. I am to take some other kind of cap or hood, so that I can pass as a Gentile.'

'It has an ugly sound, sir. I wouldn't go. Who sent this message?'

'I could get no name.'

'Then I certainly would not go!'

Solomon twisted his brown hands together. 'But dare I *not* go? I think this message comes from one of the great ones. The man was no townsman. He was from the Castle.'

'There are scoundrels in the Castle, though they style themselves earls and barons.' A few weeks' friendship with the sceptical David had taught me a good deal about the ways of the world. 'Look, sir,' I pleaded, 'with this order of expulsion every Jew is at the mercy of his enemies. You could die — you could disappear — we should be helpless! In two months there will not be a Jew in the country. Not even David would be here to ask awkward questions. A missing Jew? It would be the easiest thing in the world to make out that you had gone abroad secretly.'

For all his anxiety, Solomon could not resist a little chuckle.

'You would not make a bad scoundrel yourself, Robin. You are learning to think quickly, to see what may lie behind the surface of things. All that you say is true.' He stroked his beard thoughtfully. 'None the less, I must take my chance.'

'But what advantage . . . ?'

'Just now all my endeavours are bent to one simple purpose: to get myself, my son, my daughter — and my possessions as far as possible — safely out of this kingdom. I cannot afford to offend anyone who, as you English say, might put a spoke in my wheel. Suppose I ignore this unknown but important personage? Who knows the consequences? I need powerful friends at this moment in my life, not powerful enemies.'

I saw that. 'Is there aught I can do, sir?'

'I was coming to it. I want to ask a favour. Will you go with me tonight?'

My pulse quickened. 'Certainly, if you wish.'

He looked relieved. 'You know the possibility of danger. But I think it is much less if I do not go alone. And less still if my companion is not another Jew. That is one reason for not taking David.'

'And another reason,' I suggested with a smile, 'is that David is in no fit state to mix with Gentiles.'

'Very true. And there is yet one more reason which I must admit quite frankly.' He looked me full in the eye, gentle but challenging. 'David is my only son. He must take care of Susanna and he must carry on my family. If the worst happened —'

He did not finish. There was no need. Whatever befell him tonight — and perhaps me too — David would be left. That was important.

'You may wonder,' he went on, 'why I do not take Pierre.'

'Well . . .'

'I have a feeling that Pierre is not the right person for this evening's little adventure. He is too obviously the brawny bodyguard. A young lad like yourself will seem less suspicious — and a more usual attendant for a physician.'

It was a reasonable view. What Solomon wanted was a witness, not a bodyguard, for if really dirty work was intended no one man, even the hard-bitten Pierre, could guarantee to protect him. All the same, I had a feeling that Solomon was disclosing only part of what was in his mind.

I did not blame him. David used to say to me, 'What weapons have my people except their wits? No wonder we keep them sharp!' And the harsh experience of centuries had taught them to reveal no thought unnecessarily.

So the day passed and the evening came on. At supper the old man announced quietly:

'I have to go out tonight. I am taking Robin. We may be late, so go to bed. Pierre will open the door for us.'

'Very well, Father.' David and his sister knew better than to ask questions. They said nothing to me, even when Solomon retired to his room and left us to our own devices. David was teaching me chess. He beat me three times before the shadows gathering in the room made it hard to distinguish the pieces and I knew it was time to knock on Solomon's door.

'Is it Robin?' he called. 'Come in.'

He was writing by the soft yellow glow of his lamp. He used a wax tablet like those we had at Oxford. His hand moved from right to left, carefully scratching the curious Hebrew characters like birds' footprints on snow.

'I have finished,' he murmured. And he tilted the tablet against some books, where it would catch the eye of anyone entering. I felt sure it was a message for David, in case for any reason we were not home before morning.

'So,' he said. I helped him into his cloak. He changed his skull cap for the pointed yellow headgear he had to wear out of doors. He was not going to be seen leaving the ghetto without it. But the cloak had a dangling hood behind, so that he could remove it later. He gave me a cloth bag to carry. 'A few of my special remedies,' he explained with a smile. 'It would be foolish to go empty-handed. One never knows. And it will help to explain your coming with me.'

The courtyard was a pool of glimmering dusk, the sky overhead an unripe apple green. There was the first tang of approaching autumn in the air. A sad season, a season when things are drawing to an end. Nowhere was that truer or more poignant than in the ghettoes of England just then.

We passed forth into the street and glanced about us. Some paces away, at the corner of Lister Gate, a figure moved from the gloom beneath an overhanging thatch.

'Ah, Doctor Solomon?'

The voice was cultured, discreet, respectful. I had expected something more sinister. The messenger was a gentleman and rather elderly, I judged. Of course, he might be only a decoy.

'Here I am,' said Solomon quietly.

'And who is this?'

'My boy.' I admired his casual tone and the way he did not enter into details.

The stranger raised no objection. He thrust out a cloaked arm, like a darker wing in the darkness, and drew Solomon with him down the lane between the dyers' cottages which gave Lister Gate its name. I followed closely, stumbling over the cobbles and squelching through the filth I could not see. Over their shoulders I caught their low voices.

'I must know where you are taking me.'

'To the Castle.'

'Then why do we not go straight up Castle Gate?'

'I cannot take you in by the main entrance. I have strict orders. The visit must be kept secret. Have patience, doctor. Everything will be explained.'

'I am sure I hope so.'

We turned right down Greyfriar Gate, past the Franciscan convent which nestles at the foot of the Castle Rock. This side of the Rock is almost sheer sandstone precipice. It hung over us in the darkness, a brooding presence. On our other side there was a glint and gurgle of water. It was the Leen, a small tributary of the Trent but large enough to carry barges to a wharf the Franciscan brothers have built in front of their convent. The Leen girdles the town on its southern side and almost washes the base of the Rock at this point. Between sheer cliff and black stealthy water, I had an uneasy sense of being hemmed in.

We walked in silence. Then, at a murmured request from our guide, Solomon turned and handed me his Jewish cap. I slipped it into the bag.

If our guide was telling the truth and we were really bound for the Castle, I could only suppose that we were going to make a circuit of the fortress and enter by the postern gate on the far side. This gate must open on the park which lay west and north of the Castle. At this hour there should be no strolling townsman to notice us.

I was mistaken. Even the postern was not private enough, it seemed. Our visit must not be known to the ordinary sentries. We never reached the park.

There were, at the base of the Rock, various lean-to shelters, half huts, half caves gouged out of the sandstone behind. There was even a tavern, where a light still glimmered. Its walls and roof merged into the cliff. In the gloom it was hard to tell where building ended and natural stone began.

Just past this tavern our guide turned, taking Solomon's arm, and they vanished through a dark slit in what felt like a man-made wall. I groped my way after them. There was a smell of stables. Straw and muck were under my feet. A lantern flashed out. A fresh voice said: 'Careful, Doctor, the steps are uneven.' And Solomon answered: 'Wait for my boy; do not shut the door yet.' I saw a low arched doorway at the top of some steps and a man stooping to look back for me. His dangling lantern glittered on the rippling steel mail that covered his legs. I went up past him and the massive door was bolted after me.

Now we climbed a broad arched passage, up and up, the shadows of Solomon and our guide wavering grotesquely on the tawny sandstone. The dry nature of the rock meant that there was no dankness, no dungeon chill and no mustiness either. The air was fresh. I guessed that we were very close to the face of the precipice — we were mounting up *inside* the Castle Rock, but only just inside, so that ventilation holes brought in a draught of the clean September air.

I thought again of that night's adventure when, a few years ago, our young King Edward the Third entered Nottingham Castle secretly to surprise his mother with the traitor, Roger Mortimer. I fancy he used the route by which Solomon and I were admitted forty years earlier. But these are things it is perhaps wisest not to give away by too much detailed description, or I shall invite trouble from persons in high places.

Solomon was breathing heavily. So was I, but in my case it was not the steepness of the climb — part steps, part slope — so much as my increasing excitement. Why all this mystery, I asked myself? Who had sent for Solomon? And what was wanted of him — a cure for sickness, a love potion, a drug or poison to use against an enemy? I could not believe that Solomon would meddle in wickedness, but someone might be hoping that he would. It is not always easy to say when a doctor's true work ends and villainy begins.

There was a waft of cool autumn darkness. We stepped into a courtyard, perhaps the inner bailey. The sky hung from one row of battlements to another and it was embroidered with stars. We went up a flight of steps, a sentry passed us through the door of the keep, there were more stairs twisting up within, then a curtain swished back on its rings and we entered a chamber rosy with firelight and twinkling with candles. It was not until a little later that I was able to take in all its splendours, for I saw Solomon drop to his knees and I had just enough presence of mind to do the same.

'You are welcome, Doctor Solomon,' said the Queen.

CHAPTER SEVEN

Quest for a Good Serpent

F R O M the instant I heard the Queen's voice, doubt left me and I knew that all was going to be well.

The sweetness of her face was matched by the way she spoke. The likeness of that face, cunningly sculptured, you may still see in the great abbey at Westminster, but it is the face of a girl, with unbound hair escaping from beneath a trefoil crown, the girl whom a boy prince married long ago in Castile. That night in Nottingham I saw the mature woman, the Queen of England, but the charm remained. I saw the smiling lips and eyes that no stone-carver could depict. Above all, as I say, I heard her speak.

'Thank you, Sir John, thank you, Sir Geoffrey. You may withdraw until I need you again.'

Behind me I heard rustlings and footsteps as the two gentlemen bowed themselves out. I never caught a clear view of their faces. We were alone with the Queen except for two waiting-women who sat apart, poring over their embroidery by the light of a cresset on the wall and looking very sleepy at that late hour.

'You may stand up,' said the Queen. We got up off our knees. I was now better able to take in the scene, as I stood a pace or two behind Solomon, holding his bag.

The Queen's dark simple gown was in striking contrast with the painted cloths stiffly draping the stone walls. Very splendid these were, with rich reds and blues, bright greens and golds, portraying the adventures of the Grecian emperor, Alexander. I would dearly have liked to walk round the room, following him through all the triumphs which the ancient authors relate, but I had to face the front, swivelling my eyeballs right and left to take in as much as I could.

Soon, though, the conversation made me forget the paintings, wonderful as they were.

'You realise, Doctor Solomon, there must be no whisper of this visit?'

'I understand, madam.'

'It would alarm the King unnecessarily if he thought that I was unwell. Fortunately he has ridden off to his palace at Clipstone, to hunt in the forest, so he need not know. There are other reasons for secrecy, which you can perhaps imagine.'

'Indeed, yes, madam. You have your own physicians, who would not be best pleased to hear that you had even spoken to me! And it is my duty to remind you, madam, with the deepest respect — for the past year it has been illegal for any one of my kind to practise medicine.'

'I know. But the King is above the law. If there were trouble,' she continued with a low laugh, 'I should remind the lawyers that this must surely apply to the Queen also in such a matter, since marriage has made us "one flesh"!'

'An ingenious argument, madam! If I can help, I am entirely at your service. I am not afraid of the consequences.'

'Thank you. I am not sure that what I have to ask would even amount to medical treatment.'

'No, madam?'

'I need no doctor to tell me what ails me. It is an old sickness that has come — and gone — before. Only one

remedy is of any use, and—' she gave a little snort of impatience, the only sign she made —'the royal physicians have never heard of it! I sent for you, Doctor Solomon, because I know that long ago, like myself, you came from Spain. Tell me, do you use a strong cordial called the Golden Essence?'

Solomon did not answer for some moments. It is a doctor's instinct never to admit blank ignorance. Then he said slowly, playing for time:

'I do not use any preparation of that precise name. You appreciate, madam, the same remedy may sometimes pass under different names. The Arabs call it one thing—'

'It has the colour and the flavour of the orange. It is very potent, like fire in the throat, but afterwards comforting. A few drops work miracles.'

'You think it comes from Spain, madam?'

'I know it does. The late King of Castile, my brother, God rest his soul, sent me some. It was shortly before his death, seven, eight years ago.'

'The Golden Essence,' Solomon murmured in his beard, and I sensed from the dejected droop of his shoulders that he knew no more about it than I did myself.

She nodded. 'That was what King Alfonso called it. He had it, he said, from some learned physician at Toledo.'

'You do not know *his* name?'

'My brother never mentioned it.'

'Your royal brother, madam, was himself very well termed "the Learned". He made his court a lodestone for poets and scholars and scientists of every kind, including physicians! I am sure this Golden Essence is not generally known to my profession. If it is a secret remedy, used by one man—whose name you do not know—it will be almost impossible to trace.'

'We must try, Doctor Solomon, we must try.' There was a note of desperation in her voice. 'If only my brother were alive!'

'Is there anyone else in Toledo who could help you, madam? The present King?'

She shook her head. 'Sancho is utterly different from his father. It is not "Sancho the Learned" but "Sancho the Fighter". Everything is altered there. And you must remember, Doctor Solomon, how long it is since I left Spain — a lifetime.'

'For me, too, madam.'

'But *you* could go back — easily.'

'To Spain?'

I had to admire the tone of surprise Solomon achieved, considering how Susanna had already nagged and pleaded.

The Queen herself was now almost pleading.

'I know, Doctor, that you have to leave England. It is none of my doing and I grieve for it. But, since you must go, why not to Spain?'

'It is a great journey, madam. Costly. And, as you say, everything is altered there. I am not sure that Spain attracts me. Many of my countrymen are going no further than Paris — '

'I want you to go to Toledo. I want you to track down this Golden Essence. I need it, doctor. This time it may be a matter of life and death. You cannot refuse.'

'I do not refuse, madam, but you are asking me for a miracle. I cannot go round Toledo questioning every physician — '

'No need. Inquire among my brother's old courtiers, anyone who was near him in his last years. Ask who it was that he nicknamed "my good serpent".'

' "My good serpent"?' echoed Solomon.

'Yes,' she said eagerly. 'I have my brother's letter still, but I know that passage by heart: *"I have taken the best advice about your malady, and my good serpent sends this flask of the Golden Essence to relieve it."* The phrase struck me at the time. One does not think of serpents as good.'

'They were a symbol of medicine among the ancient pagans, madam. Your learned brother would know that. So he might well apply the words as a compliment.'

'It was deserved. That cordial cured me as nothing else could. I wish to Heaven I had a bottle now!'

My heart went out to the Queen. She spoke of that unobtainable medicine as if it were the Elixir of Life itself. I could see now that it had been more than tiredness I had noted in her face when she entered the town. She was ailing, though making a brave effort to behave normally.

'Suppose, madam,' said Solomon carefully, 'suppose I undertook this mission on your behalf — and traced the man your brother called his "good serpent" — and obtained some of his Golden Essence — '

'I should find ways to reward you!'

'It might be difficult — as difficult as my own part of the business! But my point is, madam, I should first have to bring you the medicine. Remember, after your All Saints' Day, no Jew will be able to re-enter England.'

'You could send it by some trustworthy person.' For the first time she gave me a keen stare, looking me up and down. 'Your boy is obviously English. No less obviously you trust him — or you would not have brought him with you tonight!'

'True, madam, but . . .' Solomon hesitated. He could scarcely answer that I was not available, that I was not his servant but merely acting the role for tonight. I myself dared not interrupt.

The Queen swept aside his hesitations. She fully appreciated, she said, that a journey to Spain was a great matter and that Solomon would be changing his own plans and incurring considerable expense; that she could not command him, because he was soon to be numbered no more among her husband's subjects; and that it might be difficult to reward him afterwards if he was unable to re-enter England. No matter! There must be ways and means of making the commission worth his while. Let him suggest his own terms.

It was superb, Solomon's handling of that conversation. His very silences, his diffident hesitation, his modest reluctance, all fought for him. At every pause the Queen broke in with some eager suggestion, pressing upon him some offer more than he would have dared to ask.

Clearly he must have funds for the journey and something extra for the inducements (nobody said 'bribes') that he might have to pay out for information. Clearly, too, he must have some fair reward for his services, whether he succeeded or not, and some of this at least must be paid in advance, with perhaps a later sum transmitted through the English ambassador.

'I can give you part in coin,' she said, 'and the rest from my jewel box.'

'There *is* the matter of my house,' said Solomon, with the convincing air of a man who has just had a good idea.

'Your house?'

'Here in this town, madam. As you know, our houses are all forfeit to the King. Ordinarily, we have no hope of selling them to Christians and taking the money with us — our homes must be written off as a dead loss. But you, madam — '

'I will give you the value of your house,' she said quickly. 'That is fair enough. But, Queen though I am, I had best not buy it from you. No matter. My husband will take your house with the others, openly, and I will give you its price, secretly.' She smiled. 'Agreed?'

'Of course, gracious lady! One does not bargain with a Queen.'

What else have you been doing this past half-hour, I said to myself, half amused, half angry, for like so many people before me, I had fallen under Queen Eleanor's spell.

The next day I was to find myself protesting to David: 'But it seems that your father was meaning to go to Spain all along!' And David was to answer with his subtle smile: 'Of course, my dear Robin! But was there any reason to say so to the Queen? I try to teach you when we play chess: never sacrifice any piece for nothing, always make the other player give something better in return. Don't proclaim your next move in advance. If your opponent imagines you have been forced to do something against your will, let him think so. That is the way to win.' It was not necessarily (I thought) the way to live. But, to be quite fair, a Jew had to live in Christendom as best he could. David and his father were given little encouragement to behave like knights errant in some old romance.

It was late that night when we left the Queen's apartments. The two shadowy gentlemen conducted us as before, down through the secret staircase in the Rock to the glimmering river at its base. There they murmured good night. But I fancy they dogged our footsteps till we were safe inside the ghetto. They knew that we were now in the service of their royal mistress and our lives were too precious to risk in the midnight streets.

Pierre let us into the house, barred the door and took himself off. I think he was mighty curious about the business that had kept us out so late.

Solomon smiled at me in the dim lamplight, so thrifty after the dancing brilliance we had recently left.

'You found that exciting? I can see, your nerves are as taut as bowstrings! If you go to your bed now you will not sleep till the cocks crow. I will make a drink for both of us.'

So we stayed downstairs, talking in low voices and sipping the sweet spiced wine he warmed over the embers of the fire. A white wine from Aquitaine, it was, with honey in it, cinnamon and ginger and other foreign things. And, after a few minutes, soothing as a lullaby.

'Well, Robin, you will come with us to Spain?' he said.

I had not expected this. Though the Queen had assumed it, thinking me his servant, there seemed no reason why I should. She would forget the nameless boy who had never opened his mouth. There must be other reliable ways of delivering the medicine to her if Solomon ever found it.

'You don't mean it, sir? I don't see —'

'You don't see,' he broke in swiftly, 'that it is the ideal solution? Not only for me, not only for the Queen, but for yourself?'

'I must be very dull and stupid, sir —' And by then I probably was, what with the wine and the late hour.

'Have you forgotten? You are still — what was your priest's terrible phrase, "dead to the world"? You have seen how hard it is to get the stigma of uncleanness removed. It would be far easier to start a new life, no longer Robert of Westwood but someone else, whose name has never been published as a leper. To do that safely you must make a clean break: go abroad for a time and then re-enter the kingdom in your fresh personality, merely avoiding places where your face would be remembered.'

'That would be a wonderful plan,' I agreed.

'Not wonderful, but obvious. I was going to suggest it even before tonight. But the Queen's proposal offers an easy way to put it into practice. Come to Spain with us. If our mission fails you can work your way back to England as and when you wish. If it succeeds—' he chuckled—'how better can you start your new life than with the blessing of a grateful Queen?'

Seen like that, it was a dazzling prospect. 'Do you think we shall succeed?' I asked eagerly. 'And if we do, will this medicine do all she believes it will?'

He smiled and shrugged his shoulders. 'No wise doctor makes prophecies. We shall see. As to this Golden Essence, I confess I am intrigued.' And he spoke the very words I had thought as I listened to the Queen speaking of it: 'She seems to regard it as a veritable Elixir of Life.'

Just then I could have sworn I heard a faint movement on the stairs winding up behind the curtain. Perhaps David, or more likely Susanna, had heard us and was creeping down to join us. I knew that neither would play the eavesdropper. I glanced round to see which of them would part the hangings and step into the room.

Neither did so. The curtain shivered. It could have been the draught stirring its folds. It could have been no more than a trick of the lamplight.

Afterwards, though, I remembered the incident and had my doubts.

'You will sleep now,' said Solomon. Drowsy with the spiced wine, I wished him good night and climbed the stairs. I met nobody on the way. The house was silent except for Pierre's piggish snoring overhead.

CHAPTER EIGHT

Plans and Passports

'THIS is wonderful,' said Susanna the next day.

'You have your wish,' I agreed 'Spain!'

'Yes! But I meant — that you are coming with us.'

David gave her one of his keen, calculating glances. Then he turned to me. 'I too am very glad, Robin. But for Susanna this move to Spain is particularly desirable. It is time Father thought of arranging a marriage for her — '

'I am younger than you,' she interrupted, pouting.

'That is not the point. The female ripens earlier than the male — and fruit that is ripe too long goes rotten!'

'Thank you for comparing me with fruit!'

'I am sure,' I put in tactfully, 'Susanna would not need to go as far as Spain to find a husband.'

'Perhaps not,' he said. 'But in Spain there are more of our own people, the people closest to us.'

I knew what he meant by that. Though Jews were brethren everywhere, those in Spain and Portugal formed a group by themselves, the Sephardim, while those in more northerly countries were the Ashkenazim, with differences of speech and custom.

'There is no boy in Nottingham Susanna could have married,' David went on.

'No boy in the ghetto,' she corrected him mischievously.

David, normally unshockable, looked as shocked as she had intended. 'Father would sooner see you dead at his feet than married to a Gentile!'

'And would you, dear brother?'

David recovered himself. He laughed, but grimly. 'I am more practical than Father. I think I would prefer to kill the Gentile — and not wait till he tried to marry you. Any Gentile who made love to you.'

His tone gave me the shivers. It was odd. Most of the time I lived with that family as easily and happily as if I were just another son. Then something like this would crop up and remind me that a wall stood between us, invisible but older and stronger than the wall of the Castle itself.

I was especially conscious of it on Saturdays, when everyone flocked into the synagogue. Pierre and I were the only people left in the house. We seldom had much to say to each other, but on that first Sabbath, after our journey was decided upon, he sought me out with a casual air.

'So, little clerk, you are coming with us?'

I nodded. 'You are staying with the doctor, then? I wondered.'

Pierre did not have to leave England. I hid my disappointment as best I could.

'I fancy this Spanish jaunt,' he said. 'So we shall be companions.' He grinned. With his broken nose, thick lips and craggy brows, he would have made a very passable gargoyle. 'We must stick together, little clerk. Two Christians alone among the Israelites! Look after each other, eh?'

'Of course.'

'Because nobody else will.' He added a few filthy Gascon oaths to give weight to his words. As I said nothing, he thrust his face closer, his breath rank with bad teeth. 'You went out with the old man the other night. I didn't much care for that. In the old days he'd

66

have taken me. No matter. I don't hold it against you. What was doing?'

'Didn't he tell you?' I tried to sound innocent.

Pierre snorted. 'If he had, I'd not be asking you, would I?'

'I suppose not.'

'Well?'

'Well what?'

'Where'd you go with him? What decided him all of a sudden to make it Spain?'

I backed a little, as much as I could without seeming offensive. He had me penned in a corner of the room.

'I don't know all that's in the doctor's mind —'

'You know enough to be useful!'

'He would tell us — both of us — anything he wanted us to know.'

Pierre told me curtly to stop twaddling like a lawyer. His scowl was horrific, all pretence of casual curiosity thrown aside. He was determined to find out what we had been up to that night. I was not going to tell him. And he hated me.

I have said before that Pierre was not a big man. He stood no taller than I. But he was heavier, with developed muscles and a dozen tricks learnt from scoundrels as tough as himself. He sometimes boasted of men he had killed in battle. I can believe that he had killed others less openly. In those days, I am sure, he could have killed me with his bare hands.

Once I saw a bear-baiting when the chain broke and the ferocious brute wrapped itself round the nearest spectator. Sometimes I dream of that bear and fancy myself the victim, crushed and clawed. And now, though wide awake, I felt myself in the same nightmare.

'Are you going to be sensible?' His voice was rasping

and guttural. 'I want to know, little clerk. Do I reckon you my friend or my enemy?'

I said nothing. I was all bunched up inside, ready for the roughest fight I had ever been in. The look on my face must have given him a clear answer.

The crisis never came. At that moment we heard them all coming out of the synagogue. 'All right,' said Pierre. 'All right.' And he took himself off, into the town. He was always ill at ease during the Jewish Sabbath and it was market day outside.

I said nothing immediately to Solomon. On that one day of the week he liked to be untroubled by worldly matters. The next morning I felt he ought to know.

'Pierre is very curious about our business the other night, sir.'

Solomon chuckled. 'So? But you did not tell him?'

'Oh, no, sir.'

'Good. This is the Queen's private affair. Let us keep it to ourselves, you and my own children. The sickness of kings and queens is not something to gossip about. Too many high matters of state may hang upon it. Besides,' he went on, 'as a doctor, I am vastly interested in this Golden Essence — the secret might be of great value.'

I am sure that he did not mean only value in money. Solomon was greedy for knowledge as other men are greedy for gold.

'I have been racking my brains,' he confessed. 'I have the Queen's description of this liquid. I know her symptoms, so I can deduce something from that and rule out various remedies which might look or taste the same. I am still searching through my books for a clue. I cannot find anything to fit.' He laughed ruefully. 'Not even in Ibn al-Baytar!' Seeing my blankness, he explained: 'He

68

was a learned Moorish doctor from Malaga. My father knew him. His book is called *A Collection of Simple Drugs*. But he describes fourteen hundred of them!'

'So many? I would never have thought —'

'Who in England would have thought? In pharmacy the people here are still children! I grant you, the Queen has the best available advisers. Henry Montpellier is her apothecary — a Gascon like our worthy Pierre, but rather more learned! Yet if he knew of this Golden Essence, she would not have sent for me.'

'I can see, sir, everything depends on our tracking down the man her brother called "the good serpent"!'

'Everything, Robin. And "everything" may mean more than you imagine. Think! Suppose I discover this remedy and send it to the Queen. Suppose it cures her. A queen's gratitude is always worth having — and Eleanor of Castile is no ordinary queen. She would certainly tell the King.'

'It might be a marvellous thing for you, sir —'

'Not for me only! Don't you see, Robin? Perhaps for all my people!' His gentle eyes blazed with unusual excitement. I saw his vision. The Queen's life saved, and by a Jew. The King overcome with gratitude and remorse. Who knew what the end of it all might be? The English Jews might be allowed to return from their exile.

For Solomon this search for the mysterious Golden Essence had begun to resemble the Quest of the Holy Grail in the French romances.

Why then were we not already on the road for far-off Spain?

I can only answer that this was real life, not a French romance in which knights can leap into the saddle and gallop straight off to the end of the earth without need of plans, provisions or passports.

We could not start until Solomon had cleared up his

affairs in Nottingham. Luckily, foreseeing the King's decree, he had been making quiet preparations for some time. Now, with the Queen's favour secretly helping things on (there were no more visits to the Castle but many a discreet message passed to and fro), he was able to complete his business without delay.

Thanks to the Queen's influence, he obtained a permit to land, if necessary, at Bordeaux and travel onward across the King's Duchy of Aquitaine. As King Edward had already expelled the Jews from his overseas possessions, this might prove valuable if we could find no ship sailing direct to a Spanish port.

'And here is something for yourself.' With a smile Solomon handed me my own permit to travel outside the realm. It was made out to 'Robert, clerk of Oxford', with no give-away mention of Westwood in Nottinghamshire.

I seized it gratefully. It was the foundation on which I could start to build my life anew.

'With this parchment you can wander over the world,' said Solomon. 'Who questions a poor scholar — so long as he obeys the law? "Poor",' he repeated, turning his mild eyes heavenward. 'I would rather say "rich". I envy you. You have youth — strength — no country barred to you — all knowledge and learning before you, yours to take!'

What can a boy say when an old man goes on like that? But I could see his point of view.

My document, I was glad to see, made no mention of my travelling in his party. That would not have helped when the time came to go my own way. Also, as Solomon explained, there might be occasions even before then when it was advisable to keep silent about knowing each other.

'You will see, as you journey through the world,' he

said wistfully. 'A Christian who is too friendly with our people is seldom loved by his own. I should not like you to suffer on our account.'

'I have no use for a man who denies his friends!'

'There are times when it is better for all concerned.'

It was a sad time in the ghetto, a time of tearful partings. Some familes were bound for Flanders, others for Paris, but none felt quite certain where they would find shelter and livelihood.

I could sympathise. I too had learned what it felt like to be an outcast. I too was uncertain of what lay ahead. But I was a boy, healthy, strong, ready for adventure, welcoming any excuse to see the world beyond the seas. It was not the same for the old men and women, the sick, the mothers with small children and babies to come.

King Edward, I knew, talked much of chivalry and the Knights of the Round Table. I would have liked to ask him where was the chivalry in this driving out of the helpless Jews, but if I could have met him face to face I suppose I should have lacked the courage to utter a word : only a Saint or a jester can speak the uncomfortable truth to kings, and the first Edward could be a lion in his rage. Luckily for me there was no chance of an encounter. The King was at Clipstone Palace in the heart of Sherwood, where Parliament was to meet later in the autumn, and soon the Queen joined him there.

We were to take ship from Southampton. David reckoned that if we started straight after the Jews' Sabbath (when they are forbidden to travel) we could get there before the next Sabbath began.

'Impossible!' said his father. 'It is more than a hundred and fifty miles.'

'We can cover twenty-five a day.'

'For six days? We are not royal messengers, my boy—nor an army in rout!'

'Are we not?' muttered David sourly.

'We must allow for delays, accidents, floods, waiting for ferry boats—a dozen things. You forget your sister. And I myself am no young campaigner. We must stop for the night when we find possible lodging, not ride our beasts to a standstill and then sleep in the ditch. My son is as impatient as a Gentile,' he added with a teasing chuckle, turning to me.

In the end, for protection, we joined a string of pack ponies carrying ingots of Derbyshire lead for shipment to Bordeaux. It was late September when we left Nottingham. As we filed across Trent Bridge, the river busy with barges and swans, we had to battle against the traffic entering for the nine-day fair that was about to begin—an unbroken flow of cattle and sheep, horses and pigs, merchants and quacks, pedlars and performers and tricksters of every type. And, above all, the waddling columns of solemn stupid birds from which the Goose Fair takes its name.

A small chapel to St Mary stands on the middle part of the bridge, a place where pilgrims and other travellers can turn aside for a few moments and ask the Virgin to shield them from the unknown perils of the road.

I could not pass it. With a murmured word to David, I slipped from the saddle and thrust my bridle into the fingers of a blind beggar squatting there in the V-shaped recess of the parapet. I dipped my own fingers in the holy water at the door, crossed myself and went in.

'Holy Mother of God,' I prayed in the dark little chapel, 'guard me from all dangers by land and sea, from robbers, pirates and heathen men, from shipwreck and fire and plague and all evils that may beset me. Grant us success in our business for the Queen. And bring me safely home.'

Home?

Where was 'home' now, I suddenly asked myself, as I remounted, dropped a halfpenny into the beggar's palm, and rode after my companions.

No matter. Sufficient the outward journey and the adventure, the quest of 'the good serpent' and the Golden Essence. This was no moment to worry about the return.

With a strange lightness of the heart, I rode southwards into the sun.

CHAPTER NINE

A Passage to Bordeaux

'THERE she lies,' said Pierre, and at last, after all the weary days on the road, I saw the ship that was to carry us to Bordeaux.

The *Gillyflower* was no different from several other vessels moored at the quayside, but they all looked wonderful to me, who had never set eyes on a sea-going ship before. I stared wide-eyed at their masts, tall and gleaming like giant lances, and their little castles, gay with paint and gilding, built out over prow and stern. I had not thought a ship could be so long — pictures in manuscripts make them look like baskets.

The *Gillyflower* was one of the last of the autumn fleet going out to Gascony for the new-made wine. Most ships had sailed before we reached Southampton. Few captains care for the Atlantic after mid-November.

Solomon had already struck a bargain for himself and his family. Better, he said, that Pierre and I saw the master on our own account.

I fancy, too, that there was a little matter of the King's Customs officers. We had both been given sundry small boxes and bottles to carry with our personal effects. 'Just a few of my drugs and spices,' Solomon told us airily, but I had my own ideas. Thanks to the Queen's favour he had managed, unlike the other exiles, to get a fair price for his house. He had disposed of all his bulky possessions in Nottingham and now he had sold the horses on which we had ridden to Southampton. He could scarcely be as poor as he liked to pretend, but what had he done with the purchase-money?

The Customs officers, alert to stop Jews from taking wealth out of the kingdom, would ask awkward questions. For myself, I would provoke none, but hide Solomon's boxes and bottles in my private bundle. Whatever they contained was his rightful property. If I could save him from the bullying of the King's officers, why not?

The master of the *Gillyflower* was Thomas of Milford, a massive fellow with a face like boiled leather and a shock of wild grey hair.

'A passage to Bordeaux? How many? Only two? Ay, welcome. Not many want to travel at this end of the season.'

He showed us where we could stow our bundles and stretch out at night. 'Ample room in the hold,' he explained. 'We're loading lead, and that weighs heavy so we can't fill the space. It's different, coming back. All this will be packed tight with the wine barrels.'

Pierre sniffed. 'Something else besides lead,' he grumbled. 'I never knew a gillyflower stink like this.'

The master laughed good-humouredly. 'There's wool, too,' he said, 'fresh fleeces — '

'Fresh!'

'Nay, if you're dainty, you must share the cabin under the after-castle. There's only four other passengers. Mind you, they're Jews.'

'We saw them just now on the quay,' said Pierre without blinking an eyelash. 'One of them a girl? A plump little wench, but pretty in that foreign way.'

'That'd be the one,' agreed the master. 'Just watch how you go with her!' he added, with an edge of warning to his laugh. As he strode ahead of us I whispered furiously to Pierre:

'Is that a way to speak of the young mistress?'

'Shut your gab,' he retorted. 'We've been told to act like strangers, haven't we?'

He was right, of course, but I saw no reason to overdo it. Ever since that morning when he had threatened me, we had kept up a relationship of controlled hostility. There had been no more clashes. We simply went our own ways. It was only on a special occasion, like today, that we were thrown into each other's company.

Fortunately the master of the *Gillyflower* was in a hurry to be gone. He was loading fast. God and the weather willing, he would leave on tomorrow morning's tide. Passengers would be wise to sleep on board. So Pierre and I did not have to keep up the pretence of fellowship and of not knowing Solomon and the others. By nightfall we had settled down together in our cramped quarters under the poop. The master, poking his head in, seemed thankful that we had made friends (as he thought) so easily.

Some sailors do not like to carry Jews, believing that they bring bad luck. But Master Thomas boasted that he

76

feared neither man nor devil, and would take Satan himself if the fare was paid.

'Only the food is awkward,' he confided to Pierre. 'I would not take them unless they brought their own victuals. They won't touch my salt pork because the pig is unclean, nor my salt beef lest the beast was not killed according to their laws. Only my herrings seem to be all right.'

'It would take a wise man,' said Pierre, 'to tell a Hebrew herring from a Christian.' They both laughed, and the master made us join him in a tankard of ale.

Soon we were unrolling our mattresses on the hard boards of the cabin, Susanna and old Miriam on the inside, against the bulkhead, then Solomon, David next, then myself, head to foot alternately, and Pierre sprawled across the threshold. Even that first night in harbour the autumn air came keenly off the water and there was no question of undressing. Indeed, throughout the whole voyage I had the shirt off my back only twice, and that was on deck in the heat of the afternoon, and my main object was to rid myself of lice.

The first day was pleasant, gliding down between two low green coasts, the sail spread like a great banner of red-and-white stripes, the water with its myriad glittering ripples like polished mail.

After that we had only a rare glimpse of other vessels or a far-off blur of land, and no other sign of life but the gulls screaming overhead and the fish leaping from our path.

I could not make out how the captain found his way so surely across this watery wilderness. As a country boy I knew how to use the stars as guides, but they are a poor substitute for landmarks like hills and towers — and when the skies are overcast, what use are they, or the sun by day?

Master Thomas showed me his lodestone. It was black with a lustre like metal. He rubbed the point of a needle against it, then stuck the needle through a straw to make it float, and laid it in a shallow dish of water. To and fro it swung, then became steady. Even when he turned the dish in his hands the needle came back to the same position, pointing somewhere behind us.

'That's north,' he said. 'It always points to the north.'

'Why?'

'Heaven only knows. Who cares, so long as it does?'

Not even Solomon, for all his science, could answer my question. He had no interest in navigation. He just longed for the end of the voyage. 'I agree with the old Greek philosopher, Anacharsis,' he said. ' "There are three sorts of men: the living, the dead, and those who are at sea".'

'Still,' I argued, 'if the winds continue favourable we shall reach Bordeaux sooner than if we travelled by land. We do not halt to sleep, we are not delayed by gatekeepers or ferrymen or blacksmiths —'

'True! And the days are duller in consequence.'

We had some friendly dispute about our speed. How did it compare with that of an ambling horse? The master heard us as he stood at the helm and offered to settle the matter.

'Go for'ard, right into the bows,' he bade me. 'Throw something into the water — an apple will do. There are plenty of rotting ones in the barrel yonder. Stand on the forecastle and throw it over this side, the starboard side. Then come back here.'

I obeyed, marvelling. David and Susanna smiled, sure that some joke was being played on me. I ran back to them, peered over the rail, and was in time to see the bobbing apple come drifting back and drop slowly astern.

'How many, doctor?' Thomas demanded from the poop.

'Twelve,' said Solomon mysteriously.

'And your pulse is normal? As a physician you will be certain of that!'

'Quite certain, master.'

Only then, as Solomon let his long-sleeved arms drop to his sides, did I realise that he had been taking his own pulse.

'Then it beats seventy-two to the minute?'

Solomon's bushy eyebrows went up in surprise at finding that a ship's captain shared his professional knowledge. He could only wag his beard in agreement.

'And my ship measures sixty-seven feet from stem to stern.' Master Thomas swung round and smiled down at me. 'What do your Oxford mathematics make of that, learned youth? How fast are we moving?'

Without tablets to work it out on, my Oxford mathematics made nothing of it. If it took twelve normal pulse-beats for the apple to travel the length of the ship — no, no, for the ship to travel —

I was still floundering helplessly in the most involved mental arithmetic when Solomon said quietly: 'I calculate, master, that if the wind kept the same for a whole hour together, we should travel about four and a half miles. Correct?'

'Correct,' said Master Thomas, a new respect in his voice. 'You've a fine headpiece on you, doctor, to do such a sum! I have it all set down in a table, myself.'

Solomon shrugged. 'It is nothing. But the speed is a fair speed. It is that of a good walker. If we could be sure of keeping it up, night and day, I should not grumble.'

For my part I enjoyed those days of fine warm autumn weather. Thomas would yarn for hours about the ports he had visited from Norway to North Africa, the marvels he had seen and (I felt pretty sure) a great many marvels he had not—phoenixes and salamanders, sea monsters with eight clutching arms, tribes of one-legged men, and such like. He was a fine one for yarn-spinning, that captain, but his tall stories passed the time.

During the long ride from Nottingham to Southampton, Solomon had begun to teach his children Spanish and I had joined in their lessons, which he now continued at sea. David mastered the new tongue with his usual brilliance. He had his nation's gift for languages, without which they would be lost in their perilous transit through an unfriendly world. Susanna had a fine ear and could mimic the right accent, but she had no intellectual curiosity. She took no pains to study grammar or learn words beyond the few needed for household matters.

Susanna, I said to myself, was a girl who would always get what she wanted with those dark eyes of hers. That pink little cat-like tongue would never need to struggle with lengthy vocabularies.

I have always been fascinated by new words. I took to Spanish, not with David's flair, but easily enough. It was wrought out of Latin, which I already knew, but with many other strange words which Solomon said were taken from the Moors. In Spain, it seemed, there was a mingling of languages. Many of the Moors knew both Spanish and Arabic, and the many Christians living among them in the South — the Mozarabs, as they were called — used Arabic script when they wrote Latin or Spanish. The Jews, as always, had their own language, but they had to be fluent in those of their Christian and Moslem neighbours.

Solomon had known Arabic as a boy in Seville. It would come back to him, he said, if he ever needed it. I marvelled at the skill with which he kept all these languages separate in his head, with English and French into the bargain, like a juggler catching half a dozen balls.

All this helped to pass the first few days, with a game of chess occasionally. Pierre, I was glad to find, preferred to play dice with the crew in the fo'c'sle, and we did not see much of him.

The fair weather saw us safely round the projecting nose of Brittany, but as we veered south-eastwards into the Bay of Biscay the sky greyed and there was a subtle change in the motion of the vessel. It was not stormy. It was just that the ocean stealthily developed a new rhythm, like the breathing of some scaly blue-grey monster.

It did not trouble me. I felt a sense of power, straddling the tilted deck, letting myself go with the ship as she pitched, as though I were riding some half-broken stallion. It amused me to see the rocky coastline of France climb higher and higher above the dipping bulwarks and then sink below them again as the *Gillyflower* rolled over to starboard once more.

I envied the look-out man in his breezy topcastle at the masthead, swinging right out until he overhung the yeasty water on either side. I longed to clamber up the shrouds and share his little box, but I knew Master Thomas too well to risk it. Woe betide any passenger who meddled with the working of his ship!

That night something woke me. It was as though some one had poked me in the ribs. I must have been mistaken, for, raising myself on my elbow, I saw in the moonlight slanting through the cabin door that both Pierre and David were sleeping soundly. I lay down again, but I was now wide awake. The creak of timber, the slap of waves, and the wind's fitful whine blended in a positive hubbub unnoticed in the day.

At last I gave it up as hopeless, rose carefully to my feet, and stepped over Pierre's legs.

It was a wonderful night, a night of silver. The full moon stood up like a burnished platter above the jagged velvet hem of the dark land. The very deck planks were drawn in plain black lines.

A short figure was leaning on the rail. It was Susanna. I went forward, my legs braced against the pitching of the vessel.

'Susanna,' I said quietly, not to startle her.

She did not turn her head. Her knuckles shone like ivory as they gripped the rail.

'I'm sorry,' she mumbled.

'Sorry?'

'Didn't I wake you? I touched you with my foot.' Her voice was so low I could scarcely hear her.

'No matter,' I said cheerfully. 'I am glad not to miss this sight. Look at France — under that moon! Is it Brittany still? Or Poitou?'

'Who cares?' She gulped. Her head bowed and she began to shake convulsively, as though some terrible grief had suddenly become too great for her to bear.

'Susanna!' I said, appalled, and put my arm round her.

Then I realised that she was not labouring under any mysterious and romantic sorrow. She was being most un-romantically sick.

For perhaps a minute the violent spasms shook her, then she went limp in my arms. She moaned. 'Oh, Robin! I wish I were *dead*!'

I tried to comfort her. 'You'll feel much better in a moment. Shall I wake your father? He might have some remedy —'

'No . . . no,' she said faintly. 'Just let me stay still for

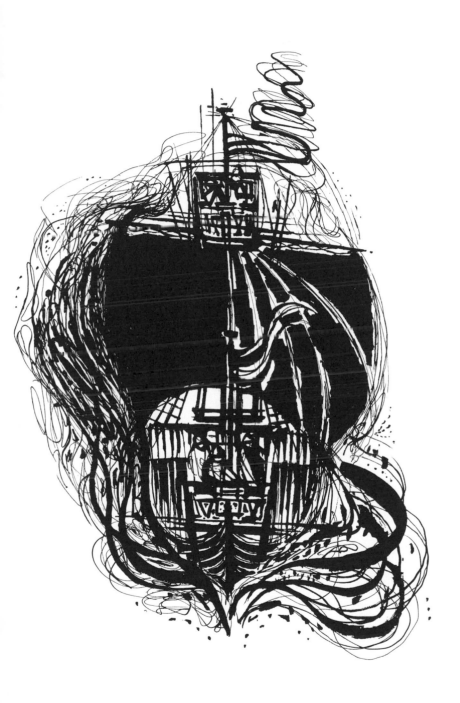

a little while . . . Then I'll go back. It's so cold here.'

We stood there, not moving, not speaking. It is not much use to make conversation with a person suffering the agonies of seasickness.

The next thing I knew was that two frenzied hands were clawing at my neck and shoulders from behind, wrenching me backwards so that I almost fell. I struck out blindly with my clenched fist, heard a gasp of pain, felt myself free as my attacker reeled away.

I expected to see Pierre, my only enemy on board. But it was David who stood there, staggering as he tried to recover his balance. The moon shone full on his lean, fine-drawn face and I saw that it was transfigured with hatred.

'So Pierre was not making it up!' he said. I saw the pale glimmer of his hand hovering over the knife at his belt.

'David,' I began, 'don't be a fool —'

A third voice broke in. It was the captain's, deep and terrible, falling upon us from above like a voice from Heaven.

'Don't draw that knife, young man — or by all the Saints I swear it will be the worse for you!' We glanced up together, like boys caught at mischief. There stood Master Thomas, high on the poop, his great paws resting on the helm. 'I tell you,' he went on, 'if any man draws a knife unlawfully on my ship, passenger or crew, there is the same penalty. His right hand is pinned to the mast with his own weapon — and he stands there till he tears himself free! I am warning you. I will have discipline.'

David glared up at him. 'Can I not protect the honour of my sister?' he demanded. But his knife remained in its sheath.

I saw it all suddenly and burst out laughing — which

84

nearly brought David leaping at me again like a demented tiger. Luckily for me, Susanna recovered sufficiently at that moment to raise her miserable head and wail: 'David, what *do* you imagine —' Then a fresh spasm overwhelmed her and she drooped over the bulwark like a wilting flower, and it became obvious even to David why I had been holding her in my arms.

He was penitent then, but I told him not to blame himself, for I knew how deeply he felt about Susanna becoming involved with a Gentile. When the poor girl had crawled back to the cabin David and I stayed on deck in the moonlight, talking in low voices, good friends once more.

'I am ashamed of suspecting you,' he said. 'I should not have listened to Pierre.'

Ah, I thought to myself. . . . Aloud I said: 'No, you should not. That man detests me.'

'I have often wondered why my father employs him. In some ways, for all his wisdom, my father can be very blind.'

When daylight came the sea grew calmer and remained so for the rest of our voyage. Susanna had no need of further comfort from any of us. But we were all thankful when one day, at sunset, we spied land on the starboard side as well as the port, and Master Thomas told us we were entering the estuary of the Garonne, with Bordeaux still sixty miles upstream but at least no more Atlantic rollers.

It was a slow crawl, that final stretch, matching wind and tide against the adverse push of the current, but on the next morning but one we found ourselves at the quayside, our long voyage over. The King's Customs officers came aboard at once. They looked sharply at my friends' yellow caps, since there had been no Jews in Aquitaine for more than a year, but they seemed satisfied with Solomon's documents and his assurance that he was merely in transit to Spain.

They scarcely glanced at me, a poor scholar with a knapsack. Pierre and I were allowed to land at once. As I acted a little farewell scene with David and Susanna, keeping my face as straight as I could, their father whispered in my ear:

'There is an inn called the Vine of Gascony. Somewhere near the cathedral of Saint-André—but Pierre will know! Wait there until we join you.'

Pierre, however, did not wait for me, and when I stepped off the gang-plank on to the cobbled wharf I could see no sign of him. That did not trouble me. In fact I was thankful to escape his company. I strolled happily along the waterfront, lined with other vessels busily loading wine, and inquired my way to the cathedral.

I found it, and the inn, without difficulty. The inn was a big place with many separate rooms opening out upon an upper gallery, which ran round the courtyard like a cloister.

Pierre had not arrived. Nor had he when, a full hour later, Solomon and his family appeared. They showed no surprise at his absence even when several hours had elapsed. They quietly settled themselves into the room they had taken, said their usual midday prayers, and prepared their meal. I ate my own dinner from a cookshop in the street and returned to the others as arranged.

Still no Pierre. And still no sign of the surprise which I alone seemed to be feeling.

Solomon pointed to my knapsack, which I had left in a corner of their room. 'Now, Robin, if you will be so good. You were carrying a few oddments for me.'

'Of course, sir.' I bent down to unpack. Then I laid

the little boxes and bottles one by one in front of him.

'Thank you, Robin. David, my son, go and stand outside the door and make sure that no one disturbs us.'

'Yes, Father.'

Solomon picked up one of the bottles, broke the seal and removed the stopper. 'This is the one I want to check,' he murmured. A pungent herbal smell, rather disagreeable, assailed my nose. It grew stronger as he up-ended the bottle and shook the dark-green shreds on to a towel. There was not much of the stuff, luckily, not nearly a bottleful. Solomon smiled at my twitching nostrils, slipped a sallow finger into the neck of the flask, and brought out a wad of tightly packed wool. Then he up-ended the bottle and shook it again over the empty part of the towel.

I gasped as I saw the glittering trickle of reds and blues and greens. That handful of rubies, sapphires and emeralds must represent a large part of Solomon's wealth.

He chuckled at my amazement. 'Now, Robin, you will understand why Pierre is no longer with us? The poor fellow must have imagined that this bottle was one of those I had entrusted to *him*. You must not be offended, Robin. I am a doctor, a man of science, and it is my method to carry out such tests.'

'It's scarcely for me to feel offended, sir! But — suppose it had been Pierre who had come to the inn and I who had vanished? How could you be sure?'

He wagged his beard sagely. 'That is another thing that goes with being a doctor. Whatever young David says to the contrary, I think I have learned how to weigh up my fellow men!'

CHAPTER TEN

At the House of Benjamin

WE'RE well rid of him,' said Susanna. Another hour had gone by and it seemed obvious that we had seen the last of Pierre. 'He gave me the shudders, that man. I never trusted him.'

'I had my doubts,' agreed her father, 'ever since the day I met Robin.'

We stared. 'You mean,' I said, 'because he was jealous of me?'

'No, no. The most devoted servant can be jealous of a newcomer — that is natural enough.'

'Then . . . ?'

'Looking back, I could never quite understand why Pierre took the wrong fork of the road — and then at once had doubts, and left me there alone in the forest — '

'I see!' burst out David. 'And the two men who tried to rob you — Pierre had fixed everything!'

'Everything but Robin's arrival! That he had *not* bargained for.'

'But you were often alone with Pierre,' I said, mystified, 'you must have travelled with him for hours — days — at a time. Why did he need any help to rob you?'

Solomon smiled. 'He had to cover his tracks. Pierre, remember, is a man with a shady record — he carries the brand on his thumb — and he dared not take chances. I always relied on that. I employed him because it was hard for one of my race to find anyone better. He worked for me because he too had little choice. So. It is finished and no harm done. He is home in his native Gascony and will doubtless find friends of his own sort. He will not trouble us again.'

'I hope you are right, Father.' David sounded less confident. 'About not troubling us, I mean. Suppose he does find friends of his own sort — and comes after us! He will not be in a very sweet mood when he has broken open your bottles and found nothing valuable.'

'We must be on our guard, my son. We shall not stay in this city a day longer than necessary — but we must find a party of honest men to travel with.'

When money talks someone will always listen politely. Though there were none of Solomon's nation left in Bordeaux or in all the land of Aquitaine and his yellow cap was stared at in the street like a flower out of season, it was not long before our arrangements were made, horses and saddles bought, and the southward road ribboning before us between the withered November vineyards.

Soon the mountains rose up in front, vast and terrible, like nothing we have in England, their heads plumed with clouds like a battle line of giants.

'We are not going over *them*?' cried Susanna, her eyes dilated with alarm. One of the merchants riding with us had sworn that these Pyrenean mountains were the haunt of dragons.

'It would be possible,' said Solomon, 'but not necessary.' He pointed towards the left. Yonder, he said, was the Pass of Roncesvalles, where Roland had died in battle with the Saracens. But the snow would soon be falling on the heights and it was too late in the year to risk the crossing. There was an easier road, squeezing between the end of the mountains and the sea. That was the way we went, crossing a sandy little river called the Bidassoa, with sea gulls screeching over our heads, and to this harsh fanfare we entered into the land of Spain.

I say 'the land of Spain', but of course it is not one realm like England. We had many bleak miles to cover before we reached the land of Queen Eleanor's girlhood. Castile is only the largest of several Spanish kingdoms. There is Aragon, which we did not see, and rugged Navarre, which we now crossed, besides the Moorish dominions of Granada in the far south. But though we were not yet in Castile itself, the great central heartland of Spain, we were at least finally clear of King Edward's territories, and I fancy my friends' spirits were lighter in consequence.

As for me, I was chiefly thankful to be out of Gascony. Whatever spiteful feelings Pierre nursed against his old master, now that he had opened the stolen containers and found them valueless, his revenge would scarcely pursue us beyond the Pyrenees.

This is no traveller's tale of foreign wonders, so I will waste no ink on that journey to Toledo. We jingled on, mile after mile, huddled in our cloaks by day, huddled over charcoal braziers in the evening. Mud and sleet are much the same in all countries.

I remember pine forests veiled in shimmers of rain. Rivers spuming over the tumbled mauve rocks. Deer drifting across heathlands as tawny as themselves. Square-towered citadels with granite walls. Churches with harshly clanging bells. And at night, last thing before sleep, the long-drawn menacing howl of wolves.

Susanna grew techy at the lack of sunshine and orange trees.

'Patience,' said Solomon, though he might have saved

his breath. 'Winter is cruel in Spain. And this is the north. In the south it is different.'

She did not like rough living, Susanna. I think travel must always be doubly hard for her people, what with the Sabbath day restrictions and the problem of getting food they are permitted to eat. In the bigger towns we found Jews enjoying prosperity and respect unthinkable in England. Here Solomon was welcomed. In smaller places it was very different. While I could gorge myself on pork or bacon, a stew of goat's flesh or whatever the inn provided, my friends had sometimes to make do with bread and cheese and such oddments as did not offend against the Mosaic Law.

'Beans!' stormed Susanna. 'I never want to see a bean again in my life. Or a dried pea. Or these bitter things.'

'Olives,' I said.

'I don't care what they're called. I'm sick of them.'

I had to laugh at her fiery indignation, but I was sorry for her. With her looks and her spirit Susanna should have been a countess at least. I can imagine that more than one earl would have been happy to make her one. But would her equally fiery brother ever agree to her marrying a Gentile, high or low?

I could only hope that she would like Spain better as time passed and that she would find happiness there. I saw that Jews and Christians mixed somewhat more freely than in England. Solomon said that this was still more marked in the south, where Christians and Moslems were also much intermingled and both communities accepted the Jew.

December found our cavalcade strung out across the icy plateau of mid-Spain, our wretched horses hanging their heads and almost leaning on the wind. Miriam fell sick. The poor old woman begged us to go on without her, though she was clearly terrified of being left to die among strangers. But the Jews do not abandon one another. Susanna nursed her as a daughter would have done and Solomon ransacked his medicine chest for remedies. We lost three days and the protection of the party we had been travelling with, but when we rode forward again Miriam was able to go with us, gallantly balancing herself on a donkey and looking more than ever like a bundle of old clothes with two beads for eyes.

In this fashion we came to the royal city of Toledo just before the Christmas celebrations began.

If you know a fine sword when you hold one, you will know about Toledo and its renowned craftsmen in steel. And in the time of Queen Eleanor's brother it had been a place of keen minds too, sharp and flexible. King Alfonso had gathered scholars and translators around him, men of all races and creeds, seeking out ancient wisdom and new knowledge, making a market-place for minds, whether in Latin or Hebrew, Arabic or Greek.

How were things now? How had King Sancho altered the atmosphere of the capital? That was what we should soon find out.

Toledo is a city of steep streets and winding alleys. It is heaped up, higgledy-piggledy, on a rugged hill. The Tagus loops it round on three sides, boiling brownly in its gorge, with a high bridge spanning it and water mills thrusting out from the rocky bank. High above stands the cathedral, which had been started sixty years before and is still building, for all I know. Solomon pointed out to me how most of the other churches had once been mosques but had obviously been altered for Christian worship. Though it was fully two hundred years since the Moors had been driven out, their memory lingered in countless ways.

'This very square,' said Solomon, as we drew rein in the centre of the city — not a square, really, but a triangular space near the cathedral. 'They call it Zocodover in their Castilian tongue. That comes from *suk ed-dawabb,* which is Arabic for "horse market".'

'Very interesting, Father,' said Susanna. 'We are not selling horses at the moment, however. Which way is the Jewish quarter, do you think?'

We found it on the far side of the city, perched on the edge of the gorge. It covered indeed all that southerly flank of Toledo, with fine houses and patios and terraced gardens. Thanks to the goodwill of the late king, and of his father before him, the saintly Ferdinand, the Jews had flourished here, holding high office and building up vast wealth and power.

Solomon had a distant cousin, Benjamin Levi, who belonged to one of the leading families. Even on that dark afternoon his house shone with colour. It was in Toledo that I began to notice for the first time the gaily patterned tiles, used freely on outside walls as well as within — a strange but beautiful custom taken from the Moors. Benjamin's house was resplendent with these tiles, with shining silver lamps and candelabra, and with warmly patterned rugs.

'Oh, this is *Heaven!*' cried Susanna, as Benjamin's wife and daughter swept her away in a flurry of welcoming fuss and chatter.

Even for me, the Gentile, there was a kind reception, especially when Solomon had sung my praises and described me as a scholar from Oxford.

Benjamin himself was a scholar, but of quite another sort. He translated Arabic books into Latin and was renowned as a poet who wrote love songs. Yet he was the ugliest little man I have ever seen, his brown face as grotesque as a carved wooden devil on a monk's choir stall. If all devils are as warm-hearted as Benjamin Levi, Hell will lose half its terror.

'Oxford?' he echoed. 'Splendid! Never, I think, have I met a scholar from Oxford. From Paris, yes, and Cremona, Salerno and Bologna — from all quarters the learned come to Toledo. Or used to come,' he added, a momentary shadow flitting across his face. Then, jovial again, he exclaimed: 'Oxford! You will have much to tell me!'

I grinned politely. It was not very likely that, at my age, I should have learned anything he did not already know.

'We hope first,' said Solomon, coming quickly to the point as soon as we had washed and been served with wine, 'that you have something to tell *us*.'

'But of course, cousin! Anything! If I can.'

'You knew the late king well?'

'So-so! He honoured many of us.'

'But you moved in Court circles — '

'You might say so,' admitted Benjamin modestly.

'Do you recall a physician — a favourite of Alfonso's, whom he called his "good serpent"?'

The little man considered, then shook his brown head. 'I cannot remember. A Jew?'

'That I do not know.'

' "Good serpent"? H'm. The phrase strikes no echo. It is difficult, cousin. The King knew many members of your craft. Despite which,' Benjamin added with a mischievous giggle, 'he has been dead these six years. More's the pity,' he went on, serious again. 'Toledo is not the same. While he lived, the learned flocked here from all countries.'

We all looked disappointed. Solomon had told us about

this famous kinsman of his. He had been sure that Benjamin would help us forward with our quest.

The little man eyed our glum faces. 'This matter is important?'

Solomon shrugged and spread his palms. 'Somewhat.'

'Then if this "serpent" exists, we will track him to his hole! I will ask around. But it may take a little time. While Alfonso lived there was a constant coming and going. One could not possibly know everybody.'

'Our "serpent", in fact,' suggested David, 'may have been a bird of passage!'

Benjamin laughed. 'Very true, my boy! And he may have taken flight when Sancho came to the throne. Many fine birds are knocked off their perches when the crown changes hands.'

Wearied by his journey, Solomon looked unusually dejected. 'I fear,' he said, 'that I have asked my question six years too late.'

'Nonsense, cousin! What are six years? We scholars can search out the truth after six centuries! Give me a few days. I will inquire. Discreetly, of course. I will put my ear to the ground.'

I nearly laughed myself, most rudely, at that. The little man's ears stuck out almost at right angles from his skull. I saw a ridiculous mental picture of him striving vainly to get one of them flat against the earth.

Now Christmas came, and for the first time for months there were whole days when I scarcely exchanged a word with David and Susanna. For months we had lived in the closest proximity on land and sea. Now they seemed to be swallowed up in this great happy community of their own people. I might have felt lonely and shut out—but it was Christmas.

'Your season of rejoicing!' cried Benjamin, clapping

his hands on my shoulders. 'And what terrible luck for you to be spending it with us who do not observe it! Never mind, my boy. I have many good friends among your people. I will say a word here and there. You will not be forgotten. Here in my house you are most welcome — but you must come and go at all times just as you please.'

In the end I spent such a Christmas as I had never dreamed of. In those twelve days of feasting I must have been bidden as guest to as many homes. Such fat geese and plump chickens and tender pigeons — not to mention the decorated boar's head that would have made Susanna screw up her pretty nose in disgust! Such sweetmeats — marzipan and ginger and almonds and figs, and at last those much-talked-of oranges, to roll fragrant in my own hands. The wine flowed free as water, though, to tell the truth, I would gladly have exchanged a whole cask of it for one quart of my mother's home-brewed ale.

Those twelve days were all drinking and eating, dancing and singing, Masses and processions, minstrels and jugglers and conjurers and acrobats. Ay, they knew how to do it in Toledo, for it was a royal capital, and the King in his palace, the Alcazar, set the tone for everyone.

'And you dance?' asked Susanna, stopping me in the patio of Benjamin's house to question me about my doings.

'Of course!'

'But they would not be the dances of your English village?'

That was true enough. The Spanish dances were slower and more stately than our lively whirlings at home, though they might have seemed less strange to me if I had been bred a gentleman. No doubt Queen Eleanor was leading just such dances in the great hall at Nottingham or wherever King Edward had moved his court for Christmas.

'A girl showed me,' I said.

That too was true. A slim dark girl named Isabella had taught me when to join hands in the ring, when to let go and clap, when to stamp which foot, when to turn right or left and follow the others round. But Susanna need not have glared at me so jealously. I had not seen Isabella again. Though they may relax for a little while during the Christmas revels, the Spaniards watch their daughters as if they were state prisoners.

Twelfth Night brought an end to these excitements — I would have said, brought life back to normal, only the next day chanced to be the Jewish Sabbath. I slept late, and you would not wonder if you had seen the last flare-up of our gaieties the night before. I awakened to a silent, empty house. Then I heard the footsteps and gentle rustle of voices as they all came flocking back from the synagogue, that beautiful pillared synagogue with its separate women's gallery, its tabernacle, and its exquisite carvings, which Benjamin had displayed to me as the pride of the Castilian Jews.

That afternoon he looked up from his book and beckoned me to his side. Though it was a bright day outside, we were all glad to gather round the brazier.

'Robin! Would you do me a small service?'

'Gladly, sir.'

'I cannot send one of my servants. As you know, on the Sabbath we are forbidden to work or to make journeys.'

'I know, sir. It is the Law.'

'I wish to return a manuscript lent me by a friend on the other side of the town. Don Rodrigo — but I think you know his house?'

'Yes, sir. I was there a few days ago. Near Santo Cristo de la Luz?'

'That is the house.' Benjamin went away and returned with the manuscript carefully wrapped in a cloth. 'My compliments to Don Rodrigo and grateful thanks. And ask him to accept this humble gift from his old friend.' Benjamin grinned as he handed me a small soft bag, very tightly laced about the neck and weighing, I suppose, about a pound. 'Warn him not to open it carelessly.'

'May I ask —' I began, feeling it nervously.

'But of course! You had better know what is inside, so that you will avoid accidents. It contains pepper.'

'Pepper!'

'White pepper. The white is somewhat of a rarity. So I think Don Rodrigo will find the gift acceptable.'

I could believe that. Even black pepper is costly enough in England. White pepper I had never seen then, though the learned Franciscan, Friar Bartholomew, mentions it in his *Encyclopaedia*, with a fanciful theory (which I now think to be nonsense) to explain why the other sort is black.

I could imagine the effect of spilling a pound of either colour. I put it very carefully into the pouch which hung at my belt, between my knife and my inkhorn.

'Good boy,' said Benjamin approvingly.

'Have no fear, sir,' I assured him. 'I will be back within the hour.'

In that cheerful forecast I was very much mistaken.

CHAPTER ELEVEN

The Mill by the Tagus

SUSANNA said afterwards that I had behaved like an innocent. But why, for Heaven's sake, should I have suspected danger in Toledo, a city that for the past two weeks had shown me nothing but the warmest hospitality?

This man caught up with me as I drew near to the cathedral. I heard the hurried patter of his shoes on the cobbles. I swung round and saw him, his cloak flying, a black shape like a raven against the orange sunset that flared across the end of the street.

'One moment, young master !'

'Yes?'

I waited.

'Excuse me! But—I thought I was right—you are the English scholar, Robert of Oxford?'

'I am. Do you want me?'

'You will not remember me. We met in a great crowd —on San Juan's Day, I think it was. But so many people, so much noise—'

To be honest, I could not remember him. In the fast-gathering gloom I made out a lean, haggard Castilian with a small beard, thirtyish, respectably dressed but not richly, neither a servant nor yet a nobleman. I had met so many new acquaintances during the Christmas celebrations, my brain had been as much overtaxed with names and faces as my belly with food and drink.

'I am sorry, sir,' I began politely.

He brushed aside my apologies. He still did not mention his own name and I did not like to ask. He seemed to be going my way, for he fell into step beside me as I turned along the west wall of the cathedral.

'I believe I can be of service to you,' he said, 'and to Doctor Solomon.'

'Can you?'

'You are looking for a serpent, I understand? A *good* serpent?'

My heart gave a jump. We were talking Spanish. I had now picked up enough of the language for everyday conversation but I still spoke haltingly and did not always catch what was said to me. So I asked him to say it again.

'A good serpent,' he repeated. 'I had better not say more in the open street, for I believe it is a somewhat private matter.'

I hesitated. 'I have this manuscript to deliver at Don Rodrigo's,' I said. 'Then I am going straight back. I could take you to Doctor Solomon — if you would be so kind — '

'It is really my master who — '

'Oh — '

'If you could spare a few minutes to visit him on your way to Don Rodrigo, that would be better. My master would be happy to tell you all he knows.'

It seemed so reasonable — what else could I have done? The man was twice my age and he was offering to do us a favour, not asking for one. Whatever Susanna said, I do not see how I could have demanded that his master (whoever he was) should cross the city to visit Solomon.

Let's be honest, I was tempted too. I should enjoy seeing my friends' faces when I marched in and told them that I had traced the person we were seeking.

'It is not far,' said the Spaniard reassuringly.

We crossed the Plaza de Zocodover. We seemed to be making down towards the Alcantara bridge, by which I had ridden into Toledo. Night was drawing its curtains round the city. After two weeks of revelry the little triangular plaza was almost deserted.

'Down here,' he said, diving into a side street between high blank walls.

'We could do with a lantern,' I muttered.

He took my arm, steadying me as I slid and stumbled. 'Not far,' he repeated.

I wondered what sort of residence lay at the end of this rough and stinking lane. Perhaps this was only a short cut.

Now I could hear a steady thunderous roar in front of us. It was the Tagus, deep in its ravine, swirling round the city in winter spate. The air grew cold and fresh.

At the bottom of the lane we found ourselves just above the river. We started out along some sort of bridge or causeway, between narrow parapets raised up on gigantic rocks. In the twilight it was impossible to make out any details. The noise made speech difficult. Peering over, I saw a white mane of water racing beneath us, a weir perhaps.

I was puzzled. Where on earth were we going? I began to dislike this somewhat odd excursion. I stiffened nervously, my steps faltering, but again I felt the Spaniard's grip on my arm.

'We are here,' he said.

A vague building loomed over us — house, watch tower, water mill — whatever it was, its foundations must be straddling the river. High over our heads one narrow window showed a slash of yellow light.

'Careful,' he said, still holding me firmly, 'these stairs are badly worn and they get slippery with the spray.'

He thrust me up ahead of him while his free hand stretched forward and pushed. A door creaked. We were inside. There was a dim diffusion of lamp-light from one corner, where more stairs went spiralling upwards out of sight. I could just make out millstones and a driving shaft coming in through the wall, but nothing was moving and I fancy no corn had been ground there for many a long day.

The Spaniard waved me courteously to the staircase.

'Straight up,' he said. 'As far as you can go. My master has made his study at the very top — you understand, he has to observe the stars.'

That sounded convincing, as if I was indeed being taken to a man of learning likely to help our inquiries. Scholars must live where their slender funds permit and a derelict water mill might be ideal for quiet study. And, though Solomon was inclined to laugh at star-gazing and horoscopes, most learned men agree that the stars influence our lives and are ignored at our peril. With the passing of years I have come round to Solomon's way of thinking — I prefer to test these theories before I accept them as true — but that night in Toledo I was still a boy who mostly believed what he was told.

So I mounted the stairs, the man following, and came breathless to a nail-studded door which looked newer and in better repair than the rest of that mouldering edifice. Again my guide reached up in front of me, but this time he knocked. A voice answered, sharp and high.

'Who is it?'

'It is I, master. Pedro. With the English boy.'

'Well done! You can come in. The door is not locked.'

The centre of the room was a pool of light, spilling from a silver lamp slung by chains from the massive beam above. In that illuminated circle stood a tall lectern with an open book. Beside it was a trestle-table, crowded with apparatus. There were glass bottles, winking brightly, flasks and cucurbits of different sizes, and retorts with down-bent necks, like marsh birds. Several vessels were connected up as an alembic for distilling.

For a moment the place seemed empty. Then I became aware of two men watching me from the shadows. They were seated either side of a brazier, its pale-red glow dimmed by the lamplight. One wore the black robe of a Dominican friar: he merged into the shadowy background, all but the pallid oval of his face. He was bald at the temples, with bushy black eyebrows as heavy and as neatly rounded as cloister arches. The other man, in contrast, was a rich figure in a fur-trimmed plum-coloured gown, with a glint of rings on his restless hands.

'So,' said the friar — and his was the rather high voice I had already heard, 'you did not have long to wait, Pedro.' Then, I thought swiftly, it had been no accidental meeting in the street. Pedro had been told to look out for me. But why? Why not a straightforward message to Solomon himself? 'Come forward, my son. You are Robert of Oxford?'

'Yes, sir.'

I advanced into the light, bowing to both in turn.

'You speak Spanish, I see.'

'A little, sir.'

'Then let us try Spanish. Don Fernando dislikes Latin.'

'It is all very well for clerks.' His companion spoke for the first time, impatiently, with the deep growl of a surly dog. I could see him better now. He was young — not that the friar was of any great age, for all his bare moon-shaped forehead. Both men struck me as curiously alert and vigorous. They gave out nervous tension as an oven radiates heat.

103

'Give the lad a stool, Pedro. A cup of wine. The air is dank down here by the river.'

I did not feel it in that upper room. The place was warm, almost stuffy, redolent of stale fumes from recent chemical experiments. I laid down Don Rodrigo's manuscript and took the wine offered me. I did not want it, but I remembered my manners. I raised the cup, murmured a respectful salutation, and drank.

'You came from England with Solomon of Stamford?'

'Yes, sir.'

'Do you know why he is so anxious to find—' The friar hesitated for an instant, then went on: 'the good serpent?'

It was my turn to hesitate. For myself I would have answered frankly, but I remembered how David and his father gave away nothing unless they had to.

'I do not know all the doctor's private business, sir.'

'Why do you travel with him?' demanded Don Fernando. 'You are a Christian? You're not his servant?'

'Wait.' The friar put out a restraining hand. 'Do not bully our young friend. He is only a boy.'

'That's what I mean, Zapata! You beat about the bush as if he were a visiting ambassador. *I* can see he's lying. He knows perfectly well why the Jew is looking for Ibn al Razi—'

'And will tell us, if the matter is properly put to him.' The friar's tone was silken, but it had the concentrated power of a strangler's cord. The young nobleman stopped in mid-sentence, almost as though he had literally felt a cord about his throat.

The friar's face was transformed, for an instant, by a spasm of suppressed fury. I knew why. Don Fernando had let out the name of 'the good serpent'. And this had not been in Friar Zapata's plan. He too must be a man who did not believe in giving away anything for nothing.

Ibn al Razi . . . a Moorish name . . . I must memorise it.

'I think there's some mistake, sir,' I said, getting up and setting the wine upon the table. 'I came because the gentleman here said you had something to tell me. But there is nothing that *I* can tell *you*, so, if you will excuse me, sir—'

'Sit down.' This time Friar Zapata directed that strange controlled power of his at me. With two quiet words he pushed me down on the stool again, yet without stirring from his own seat. 'There is much that you can tell us. And it will pay you to do so. Don Fernando is a great lord in Castile—he can do much for you—'

'Favours must be earned,' the nobleman muttered.

'And you can earn them easily,' the friar assured me. 'First, it is true, is it not? This Solomon has come to Spain because he has heard something? He has heard that another physician—let us still call him "the good serpent"—has discovered what every scholar has dreamed of discovering since Time began? The Elixir of Life?'

It was all I could do not to laugh in their faces.

How on earth had they got hold of this fantastic notion?

Solomon had told me that he did not believe in such things, though he admitted that many worthy men did. He thought it a great pity that they should waste their time and talents seeking for a preparation that would enable a man to live forever and to transmute base metals into gold. There was no evidence of any substance existing that would perform either of these wonders, and it seemed against all reason that the same stuff should serve both purposes. Wise men, said Solomon, should study Nature, test everything, and observe results. That way they might hope to improve the art of healing, step by step.

He was the last man to go chasing across Europe in quest of the Elixir or the Philosopher's Stone or any other such magical secret.

'What are you grinning at?' snarled Don Fernando.

'I beg pardon, my lord. But there *is* some mistake. The doctor has no such idea in coming here.'

'Do not lie to us,' said Zapata. 'We know otherwise.'

'Then you know more than I do, sir.' Again I got to my feet. 'You must ask the doctor yourselves. There is nothing I can tell you, and no point in my staying here. But if you have any message for him . . . ?'

My one idea, by this time, as you can well imagine, was to get out of this place. I was keenly conscious of Pedro, silent behind me, his back against the door.

'I have no message for the doctor,' said Zapata slowly, 'but I have something to say to you.'

'Sir?'

'Listen well. Consider. You are on the wrong side in this business. Yes, *"side"*. For Don Fernando and I are in it now. We can make better use of this secret than your Doctor Solomon. You must see that. You are of our faith. For.that reason alone I give you this solemn instruction: it is your duty to aid us rather than this unbeliever.'

'We can also make it very well wórth your while,' said the young nobleman.

The friar ignored this crude interruption. 'You will take an oath of secrecy before you leave here. You will return to Solomon and breathe no word of this meeting. You will stay with him and pick up all the information you can. This you will pass on to us. We shall arrange a method with Pedro here, and he, at the same time, will pay you for your help. You understand?'

'I understand, sir.' I played for time. I was now badly frightened. This was an evil place. The two faces studying me were evil. The shadowy room was full of menace. 'May I think about this a little while? Perhaps tomorrow morning — after Mass — outside the cathedral —'

'We are not children,' said Zapata. 'You will take a sacred oath now.'

I swallowed. 'Then, sir, I must decide now. I cannot.'

'Cannot?' Don Fernando sounded incredulous.

'Cannot, my lord. I owe a great deal to Doctor Solomon —'

'Has he *converted* you?'

'Of course not, my lord! Nor even tried. But I cannot spy upon him.'

Don Fernando swore horribly and started to his feet.

'The young puppy means it,' said Zapata.

'I can tell he does!'

'Then what do you —'

'I am going to throw him downstairs before he annoys me any more!'

'No,' said Zapata. 'He must not run off to Solomon with this story.'

'He won't run anywhere!'

'But even if he breaks his neck there will be gossip and suspicion — which you know I can ill afford!' I was backing away during this agreeable discussion, but Pedro's arms clamped round me and held me powerless.

'We can't let him go—just like that,' protested Don Fernando.

'We can't let him go at all,' Zapata corrected him. 'He knows far too much. Thanks to your carelessness!'

'*My* carelessness?'

'Not only can he tell the Jew that we are interested in this business — he can now tell him the name of "the good serpent"!'

Don Fernando cursed again. 'I did not think! I was so sure the boy would come over to our side. Never mind. That is easily put right.' He laughed in a way I found very far from amusing.

'Yes,' said Zapata, 'but it must be arranged carefully. This Solomon has important friends in Toledo. There will be questions. There must be nothing to connect us with the affair — or this place.'

'The river will take care of that difficulty!'

'True.' Zapata turned to Pedro, who had shifted his grip and now had my arms twisted behind me. 'Listen, Pedro. You will lock this boy in the room below —'

'And then?'

Zapata smiled. His black eyebrows went up. 'You must read my thoughts. My conscience will not allow me to say more. Do nothing for a couple of hours — until, let us say, you hear the monastery bell ringing for compline. By then, Don Fernando and I will have shown ourselves elsewhere — established what the lawyers call our alibi. After that —' He shrugged his shoulders. 'The less he and I know about it, the better.'

'I won't do it,' said Pedro surprisingly. His voice, vehement with emotion, was almost at my ear as we stood there, locked together.

'Won't?' echoed Don Fernando.

'No! Poor I may be, but I am a gentleman, not a murderer! I brought you this boy as you asked, but I had no idea —'

'You have no idea of what is good for you,' said Zapata unpleasantly. 'No matter! We can do without you — from now on. Let us hope that *you* can do without *us*.'

'Easily!'

Pedro released me with a push. Before I could recover my balance Don Fernando was upon me. I struggled, clawing for the knife at my belt, but my fingers touched only an empty sheath. Pedro must have disarmed me earlier.

He had gone now. The door creaked and swung, his footsteps were fading down the stairs.

'We'll lock him in the room below,' said Zapata, 'and proceed exactly as I said.'

'Pedro won't come back, though —' Don Fernando was panting and gasping with the effort of holding me and dragging me across the room.

Zapata laughed. 'Turn "Pedro" into French — you get "Pierre". I think our new Gascon will be more obliging. And less squeamish.'

I fought on every stair as they hustled me down, but I had no chance. Another door was flung open. They threw me inside, banged it in my face, and shot the bolts. I was in darkness but for a glimmer of lamplight through a small grating in the upper part of the door.

Their voices died away as they continued down the stairs. Now there was silence except for the thunder of the river boiling past the foundations of the mill.

CHAPTER TWELVE

Elixir of Death?

PIERRE!

I began to see a glimmer of meaning in this tangled affair.

The friar had spoken of 'our new Gascon'. That could only be Solomon's former servant. He must be here in Toledo, having followed us all the way from Bordeaux, cursing the folly that had tempted him to desert with those valueless bottles.

If he had not shown his hand then, he would still have been travelling with us, able to spy upon his master's private business.

That, I now realised, was what he had done at Nottingham. I remembered how inquisitive he had been about our visit to the Castle. Now, casting my mind back, I recalled how Solomon and I had talked that night before going to bed.

Solomon had spoken of the Queen's pathetic faith in the Golden Essence. 'She seems to regard it,' he had said, 'as a veritable Elixir of Life.' And at that moment I had heard a faint sound on the stairs, and expected David or Susanna to fling back the curtain, but nobody had appeared.

So Pierre had heard, or rather half-heard, our conversation.

He had jumped to the mistaken conclusion that we were really on the track of the Elixir of Life. The man who discovered such a secret would have the world at his feet. He would have power and wealth beyond the dreams of kings or popes or emperors.

A man like Pierre would not delude himself that he could exploit the priceless secret alone. He had not the chemical knowledge. Nor had he the contacts with the great ones of the earth so that he could bargain to the best advantage.

This much was clear then. He had shadowed us to Toledo. He had found ideal patrons — or partners — for his enterprise. Friar Zapata was obviously a keen alchemist with a well-equipped laboratory. Don Fernando was a grandee with access to the King of Castile. A well-balanced trio, and, I thought grimly, from what I knew of them, well-matched in villainy.

And it was all a mistake! He was leading the two Spaniards upon a wildgoose chase. For even if such a thing as the Elixir of Life existed, it was certainly not what we were hoping to obtain from — what was 'the good serpent's' actual name? Ibn al Razi?

It should have been funny. But it wasn't. How could I convince them that Pierre was utterly mistaken? I should not see the men again — I should only (if I had understood their parting words correctly) see Pierre himself, and that all too soon. Even if he believed me, he would not want the others to learn the disappointing truth.

The Elixir of Life looked like proving, for me at least, an Elixir of Death.

I studied my prison in the pale light streaming through the grating. The door opened outwards, but though I bruised my shoulder hurling myself against it, I could only make it rattle. The room was empty: there was not even a stool I could use as a battering ram. My knife had gone. I had only my pen knife with its tiny blade, fit for nothing but sharpening quills. Nothing less than an axe would have been much use against the massive timber of that door.

I worked my way round the walls, checking that there was no other way out. There were some narrow slit windows in the masonry, but not even a dog could have wriggled through, and I reckoned there must be a considerable drop outside. A change in the sound of my own footsteps led me to stoop and examine the floor. My heart beat wildly as I realised that there was a trap door, which creaked open as I wrenched back the rusty bolt and lifted.

No good! Below me — sickeningly far below me — was the frothy flood of the river.

'Do not try it,' said Pierre. 'The Church tells us that suicide is a grave sin.'

I glanced over my shoulder, and there he was, leering at me through the little barred opening in the door. I let the trap thump back into place and went over to him.

'We meet again,' he said, 'but I think this *is* the last time.'

'Let me out, Pierre,' I pleaded. 'Murder is a sin too. Haven't you enough on your conscience already?'

'I can get pardon for sins.'

'What harm did I ever do you?'

'I have killed many a man who did me less,' he said in an offhand tone. 'And there is the future to think about. Friar Zapata tells me you know more than is good for you.'

I looked into his eyes. I saw no mercy there. For a moment, I freely admit, my nerve cracked. 'Then for pity's sake,' I burst out, 'do it now! Get it over! Don't make a torture of it!'

If only he would open the door! Unarmed, unequal in every way, I knew I had not one chance in ten against him. But better a short, hot-blooded struggle and a quick end than this agony of waiting.

He made no move to slide back the bolts. He chuckled, savouring my fear.

'No hurry,' he said. 'When we hear the monastery bell will be time enough. Perhaps their evening prayers will help to lift your soul Heavenwards? Your carcass will certainly go in the other direction. Handy, that trap door.'

In the next hour I learned just how much he hated me. Pierre was a curious, distorted person. He hated Solomon and all his family, as men often will hate those who have been most generous to them. But me he hated especially. From the day I stepped into his life, upsetting the scheme to rob Solomon in Sherwood Forest, he blamed me for everything that had gone against him.

To his flow of threats and mockeries I made no answer. His words, filthy beyond repeating, ran on like the gutter in a city lane. When he paused to take breath and scrape his mind for some bloodcurdling obscene gibe as yet unspoken, there was quiet except for the throb and swish of the torrent far beneath my feet. I closed my ears and my thoughts against him. I prayed and prepared myself for the death that seemed certain.

Pierre had a fine new dagger of the famous Toledo steel. He had not failed to mention it or the purpose for which it would soon be used. I had only my belt, a light girdle without metal studs or anything that would transform it into a weapon.

Wait, though! As my desperate fingers tested it I was suddenly reminded of the pouch that hung from it, unusually heavy. Heavy . . . but not all that heavy. Even swung from behind, upon the skull of an unprepared opponent, it was not enough to give more than a harmless thump. And Pierre was anything but unprepared.

He was not prepared, though, for the contents of the bag which bulged my pouch. A good pound of pepper! It was lucky that I was standing well away from the door so that Pierre could not see the joy in my eyes as I realised that I now had a good chance of life.

The remainder of that waiting time was almost worse than what had gone before. At all costs I had to hide my new feeling of hope. I had to act the helpless rabbit, paralysed by the watching stoat. I had already given up replying to the Gascon's taunts. He saw me only as a shadowy figure skulking against the far wall.

I suppose my silence irritated him. I was not giving him the satisfaction he had expected. He grew bored with the one-sided conversation. He seemed as glad as I was when the distant monastery bell clanged above the deep rumble of the river.

'I hope you have said your own prayers?' he said, and slid the bolts.

I had already considered how best to meet him. I could make a wild rush — he would half expect that — and hope to throw the pepper in his eyes before he got too near. Or I could cower back in the shadows, another natural way for a doomed victim to behave.

That was the course I chose. I had taken up my position on the far side of the trap door. As Pierre stepped into the room, slowly and deliberately, his dagger naked in his hand, I opened the trap at my feet.

There was thus a yard square gap yawning between us, and the flap, tilted back on its hinges, doubled the obstacle. This meant that he could not rush me. He must come round either from the right or from the left, or he would have to jump the obstruction. Whatever he did, I should get a moment's warning of his intentions.

He, luckily, had no inkling of mine, no suspicion that I had any defence against him. Knees bent, head hunched, arms spread, a silhouette against the lighted doorway, with only the Toledo steel glinting in contrast, he moved inexorably towards me. I was glad I could not see his face. For all my new-found hope it might have unnerved me.

'Come to Uncle!' he coaxed me. 'Or must Uncle come and get you?'

He was very sure of me. However I dodged and swerved, he was confident I should not get past him. And in the ordinary way I doubt if I could have. Pierre was amazingly quick on his feet, and his long arms could flash through the air like grapnels.

He advanced to the edge of the open trap. He saw that pathetic inch-long blade of my penknife. He lifted his head and roared with laughter, thinking that I was going to pit it against his dagger.

'So you are armed after all! Come on, then! Let us fence!'

That was my moment, as he stood there, feet apart, rocking with amusement at his own wit, confident that the trap door defended him as much as it defended me.

I slit the bag and threw it. He took the pound of pepper full in the face.

Even I was blinded for the time being. But I had thought out my escape route and forced myself to follow it, eyes smarting, coughing and sneezing uncontrollably, while the Gascon howled and writhed like a fiend.

I groped my way round the wall, then, knowing myself safely past the open trap, rushed for the door. I was through! Tears streaming down my cheeks, spluttering and gasping, I slammed the door, clawed wildly till I felt the bolts, and then shot them into their sockets. I could still hear Pierre agonising on the other side.

When I could see properly, my first instinct was to run down those stairs as fast as I could. Then I remembered Don Rodrigo's manuscript. Though I was not going to deliver it tonight, why leave it on Zapata's table? My eyes burned but my brain had gone strangely cold. I knew that there was no risk of the friar's returning for some time. He and Don Fernando were too busy establishing their alibi.

I took the lamp off its shelf and went up the stairs instead of down. The manuscript was lying where I had left it. I thrust it inside my tunic. Then, placing the lamp carefully on one side, I set to work as though a demon had entered into me. Perhaps one had.

I wrecked everything in sight—except the books. No scholar could have done that, though I wonder now if they may not have been full of devilry and better burned. But all those flasks and retorts I dashed to fragments, and all the powders and crystals and liquors they contained, till the floor was a multi-coloured stain, a crunching shingle of jagged glass.

Then, my fury suddenly spent, my breath coming in great sobs, I picked up the lamp and fled downstairs. Pierre bellowed at me through the grating—I caught one glimpse of his blood-shot eyes as the lamp's beam flitted across the door in passing. A minute later I was outside in the clean January darkness, hurrying uphill towards the lights of Toledo and the overhanging stars.

CHAPTER THIRTEEN

The Marble Forest

'Zapata?' said Benjamin. His kindly, ugly face looked grave. 'You are well out of *his* clutches, my boy.'

We sat up late that night, you may imagine, while I told of my adventures at the mill and we discussed the business in all its aspects.

'It sounds,' said Solomon, 'as though this friar had a certain reputation?'

'He has,' agreed the little scholar grimly. He looked at me. 'I am not one to criticise Christians to their fellow Christians, but in this case I do not think Robin will be offended! He has learned tonight, if he did not know before, that not every man is holy by the mere putting on of a religious dress.'

'I am not a child,' I said. 'I can believe anything of Zapata.'

'He is, in fact, in disgrace with the Church authorities. He has been disciplined by the Dominican Order. They disliked some of his scientific investigations.'

'They would!' For a moment I felt a passing sympathy with Zapata, despite my recent rage against him. 'There is an old Franciscan at Oxford,' I explained. 'They say he is the most wonderful of scientists, but he's been persecuted all his life and he is practically a prisoner, though he is nearly eighty —'

'We have all heard of your learned Friar Bacon,' Benjamin interrupted with a smile, 'but I doubt if even his unusual ideas give as much cause for offence as Zapata.'

'What does Zapata do, then?' asked Susanna.

Our host's smile faded. 'Some years ago he dabbled in the study of medicine. He wished to understand the structure and internal workings of the human body. But, as no doubt you all know, the Church is against surgery and forbids the dissection of a corpse for medical study.'

'The Church is wrong there!' I burst out impulsively. In that company I could say what I thought.

'Very likely,' said Benjamin in a polite neutral voice. 'But it was rumoured in Toledo that Zapata had gone considerably further than the secret cutting open of the dead. He decided that he could learn more if he began his anatomical studies while the body was still alive and functioning —'

'*No!*' cried Susanna in horror. I felt a wave of nausea. So this was the kind of man I had just escaped from!

'It may be gossip,' said Benjamin. 'But certainly the friar is under a cloud. You can understand why he dared not risk being connected with Robin's disappearance. And another thing: he is a man of immense ambition, now barred from the Court and frustrated in a dozen ways. Imagine what it means to him, this story your Pierre has brought him! He believes in the Elixir of Life, he believes that you are on the track of it. What a temptation to him! And to that arrogant young scoundrel, Don Fernando!'

'One thing I don't understand,' said Susanna.

'My dear?'

'If they think that this Moorish doctor already *has* the Elixir of Life, what do they suppose he is doing with it? Why hasn't *he* made himself master of the world?'

Benjamin laughed till he shook all over.

'My dear! If you had met Ibn al Razi! I knew him only slightly during his stay in Toledo — not enough, even, to have heard the pet name the old king gave him. But he *was* a "good serpent", quiet and wise and unnoticed. To men like Zapata and Fernando he would seem an unworldly old fool, a man who might make a priceless discovery yet never think of putting it to any profitable use.'

'And you think he now lives in Cordova?' said Solomon.

'So I hear. Which means, I suppose, you will soon be on your way there?'

'We must not lose a day.' The doctor's vehement tone drew all our eyes upon him. 'Don't you see,' he went on earnestly, 'that this matter is even more urgent than before? It is no longer only a question of medicine for the Queen. Ibn al Razi must be warned. He is in grave danger. These men have failed to win Robin to their side. Surely, now, they will make a bee-line for Ibn al Razi himself?'

'But if he hasn't the Elixir — ' I began, and stopped, realising what Solomon feared. 'Of course,' I added lamely, 'whatever he tells them, they won't believe him.'

'*You* should know that,' said David. 'These men do unpleasant things when they think that someone is holding back information. Obviously, they would gain nothing by killing him. But there are worse things than being killed.'

'How far is Cordova?' asked Solomon. 'A hundred miles? A hundred and fifty?'

Benjamin shook his head. 'I would think nearer two hundred. And this is the worst time of year. The sierras are deep in snow. It will take many days.'

'All the more reason to start at once! At dawn, if possible, when the city gates are opened. Can you help us, old friend? I am sorry to leave you at such short notice, but you understand?'

'Of course, of course! Ibn al Razi is in danger. So are you all.'

'Especially Robin,' said David, 'once Zapata sees what has happened in his study!'

'That,' said his father, 'is another reason for getting out of Toledo by first light. With luck, Zapata will not go near the mill until tomorrow. That would be natural, if he is concerned to establish his alibi.'

'And Pierre will be cooling his heels till then,' Susanna remarked with considerable satisfaction. 'Do him good!'

Benjamin gave orders to his servants. Horses and guides were to be ready before dawn. There was no question of old Miriam travelling further with us. It was agreed that she should stay in the shelter of Benjamin's household. Susanna was invited to do the same, but she flatly objected.

'But a girl will slow us up,' protested her brother.

'I can ride as hard as Father!'

'But—'

'Do you think I am going to stay in Toledo alone— where all these terrible things happen?'

Susanna did not sound like a timid girl, but she was ready to use any argument that suited her. And there was enough sense in it to make her father waver. True,

Benjamin was a man of influence and she *ought* to be safe enough under his roof. True, neither Zapata nor Fernando was in favour with King Sancho, so they had to watch their step and could not openly break the laws of Castile. None the less, the friar was ingenious enough to find some means of striking at Susanna. Left in Toledo, even in the apparent safety of the Jewish quarter, she was a possible hostage to the enemy. I saw that her father would not feel happy in his mind. Sure enough, Susanna got her way.

The belfries of Toledo were rocking, the wintry dawn kindling fiery red behind them, and the first sleepy-eyed churchgoers shuffling to Mass as we rode out across the San Martin bridge that Sunday morning and took the frosty road southwards.

There were six of us. Benjamin had provided us with two stalwart servants, Isaac and Aaron, as guides, grooms and bodyguard. David, his father and I had swords and daggers too. We should be able to defend ourselves, whether against robbers on the way or against any pursuers sent by Zapata. There was no time to waste in joining some slow convoy which might not start until Monday or even later. Our own speed was our best protection.

It seemed strange to me at first that our journey had suddenly taken on this new urgency — as though the life of an unknown Moorish doctor were more important than the Queen's. Of course, it wasn't so. It was just that Ibn al Razi's danger was immediate. In his case a day might make all the difference. We had never expected to supply Queen Eleanor with her Golden Essence until some time in the spring. We realised now that she might never receive it if Zapata and his friends reached al Razi before we did.

Moor, Jew, Christian . . . What difference did it make?

'He is a man,' said Solomon, 'a good man, a man of science and learning. Is his life nothing in the eyes of God?'

Months ago, in the Nottingham ghetto, I had come to accept Solomon and his family as true friends, to understand their different ways and to discover that in many other respects there were no differences to divide us. Should I now find it the same with the Moors — people I had grown up to think of as far-off outlandish infidels, kin to the Saracens whom King Edward had warred with on his crusade? Certainly the Spaniards often spoke of them with admiration, and I had an idea that Benjamin and most other Toledo Jews privately considered the Moors more civilised than the Christians.

There was time to think about such things as we rode southwards. What I tell in a few lines took days of hard travelling in reality. Just because we were always conscious of Zapata's shadow behind us, it must not be imagined that we thought of nothing else, or that we galloped hell-for-leather those two hundred miles, our heads twisted back over our shoulders to watch for pursuit. That is very well in romances. In real life, on a Spanish road, you would soon break your horse's neck and your own.

No, we went doggedly on, keeping our eyes open, making all possible speed, but seldom speaking of the dangers at the back of our minds. Instead, we joked as usual, argued and teased Susanna, and whiled away the unavoidable halts with discussions on every subject that interests the human intelligence.

It was a bleak, high country. We passed few towns of any size except Villa Real, the 'royal city' founded by the learned King Alfonso fifty years before. There was snow everywhere. The bones of the land stood out through it, brown and grey, like a skeleton under a tattered shroud.

We paused to sleep and to have our mounts shod. But always we pressed forward without losing a day.

'But tomorrow,' I reminded David, 'is surely your Sabbath?'

'It is. But this is a matter of life and death. So the Law permits us to travel.'

Before the second Sabbath came upon us we looked down from a hill and saw, stretched along the bank of the broad Guadalquivir, the vast city of Cordova. Solomon's eyes shone as he pointed. 'Yonder,' he said, 'the pride of Andalusia!'

'I have heard of Cordova leather,' I said. 'It is famous even in England.'

Solomon gave a comical groan. 'A true Englishman's remark! Cordova leather — Toledo steel — Bordeaux wine! You will grant a little admiration to the foreigner if he produces something you can use. My dear Robin, Cordova is famous for something more than shoes and saddles!'

As we rode on he told me, regret in his voice, of the city's greatness under the Moors, fifty years before.

'They had made it the Baghdad of the western world! My father used to tell me of its wonders — our own Seville, remember, is only seventy miles down-river from here. Seville was splendid in those days, but Cordova — ah, Cordova! It was a city of palaces. The Palace of Flowers, the Palace of Pleasure, the Palace of Lovers, the Palace of Damascus —'

I stole a glance at Susanna riding beside me on a white mule. She was rapt in visions of the past — and doubtless comforting herself with the thought that at least some of these ancient glories must remain.

Now that we had come over the last of the central

sierras, out of Castile and into Andalusia, Spain was beginning to live up to her expectations. Solomon had promised that here the spring came early. It was true. There was a caress in the very air, with pink almond blossom outspread against a backdrop of blue silken sky, green leaves opening, and every tree a minstrels' gallery of birds.

I only half listened to her father, going on about the splendours of Cordova before the Christians took it.

'Three thousand mosques! Three hundred public baths — like us, these Moslems are a clean people. You doubt the numbers? When I tell you the population of the city — half a million in those days! Is there one-tenth that number in London?'

'Look, Father!' Susanna interrupted. 'Oranges!'

We looked, and the present wonder of the tree made me forget the bygone marvels of Cordova. It shone and glowed in the sun — creamy white blossoms, pale unripe fruits, hot golden spheres of ripe ones, all mingled miraculously amid the glossy evergreen foliage.

'Oh, the *scent*!' cried Susanna. She wheeled her mule and rode straight into it, eyes shut, face lifted to brush the boughs. I did the same. I flooded my lungs with the sweet fragrance.

From the roadside her father called impatiently: 'You will see them everywhere! Wait till I show you the great mosque of the Caliph, and the Court of the Orange Trees! Hundreds of them in ranks, matching the marble columns inside — '

We turned back to him, almost with reluctance, and continued on our way.

Solomon assured us that the Christian conquest had been the ruin of Andalusia. Towns and countryside alike had decayed under the rule of the Castilian kings. It was a dry land in summer, he said, though we might find that hard to believe now after the snows and rains of winter. Only the Moors, remembering the African deserts from which they came, knew the preciousness of water. With tanks and dams and sluices and channels they had learned to hoard it and dole it out again through the torrid summer days. They had turned Andalusia into a vast orchard and garden. We could see for ourselves, if we looked to right and left of the road, how the land had gone back under its new rulers. The Castilians did not understand irrigation.

I listened politely. When you are young, you have to listen to the old. It is part of the debt you owe to life.

But what the devil, I thought rebelliously, had all this got to do with me?

How could I be expected to interest myself in irrigation when Cordova lay before us and, if we were lucky, the end of our quest?

By tomorrow perhaps we should have traced al Razi. I might be starting back for England, bearing a flask of the Golden Essence to the Queen.

I was braced for adventure. And steeled against the knowledge that, if things went to plan, it would also mean saying good-bye, probably forever, to Solomon and David and Susanna. I felt it in my bones that, even if the Queen's gratitude wrought some miraculous change of heart in King Edward, they would never wish to return to England. Susanna least of all.

The bright clean air of Andalusia deceives the eye. Though the white, tree-bowered city had seemed close to us, there were some miles still to cover, and we reached it only as the gates were about to shut and the waters of the Guadalquivir were wine-red with the sunset.

We made, as usual, for the Jewish quarter, in the far

corner of the city, between the royal palace and what had once been the great mosque of the Caliphs, close to the river. There had been a time, said Solomon, when the Jews had practically run the affairs of Cordova under the Moorish régime. The Kings of Castile had clipped their wings. Though still powerful and prosperous — still far too useful to do without — they had been penned inside a ghetto. Benjamin had given us an introduction to Samuel Sharada, one of their leading merchants.

I must say that, after the unpleasant episode in Toledo, I did not mind sleeping behind the extra protection of a ghetto wall.

True, we had seen no sign of pursuit on our journey, and now, even if we had enemies hard on our heels, they could not overtake us before tomorrow at the earliest. All the same, there was something reassuring about the ghetto. It was like a citadel.

Sharada knew all about Ibn al Razi. The doctor lived quietly with his granddaughter on the northern side of Cordova.

'In the morning,' he promised, 'I will send one of my servants to guide you to his house.'

Solomon looked more relaxed than I had seen him for days. It was hardly surprising. The journey from Toledo had taxed his strength, and he was (he admitted) getting too old for these adventures. He was thankful that now the end was in sight. Once he had found al Razi and persuaded him to supply the Queen's medicine, his own part would be done.

'You will not misunderstand, Robin,' he murmured to me privately, 'if I go to see al Razi alone?'

'Of course not, sir!' I tried to keep the disappointment out of my voice. 'Why should I?'

'Because you have been a faithful companion in this

matter from the beginning — and you are going to complete it for me. But this first visit to the Moor is a little delicate.'

I laughed. 'One doctor asking another for his special remedy?'

'Oh, al Razi is not like that, by all accounts! I am confident he will agree. But, as you say, it is an affair for the two of us. I shall not take David either. When all is settled you shall both meet this "good serpent" we have sought so long! He may give you some instructions to deliver with the medicine.'

'I only hope — ' I began and paused.

'Yes, Robin?'

'That you will not take risks by going alone?'

'Our kind host is sending one of his men to guide me. Aaron can go too. Servants can be left at the door. You and David could not be. I know what is in your mind.'

'I am sorry, sir. But since Toledo I have been wary. It isn't Pierre, it's this man Zapata. Something uncanny . . . Once you've seen him at close quarters you feel that anything might happen.'

'I shall be careful. And I shall give al Razi the strongest warning. No doubt he knows all about Zapata and will need no persuading. You feel happier now?'

'Yes, sir. But while you visit al Razi I shall go and hear Mass — I have been slack in my duties of late. And I shall offer a candle to the Virgin and pray that she continue to protect us.'

'Do that,' said Solomon gently.

So, early the next day, I found myself in the renowned Court of the Orange Trees with David and Susanna. The great quadrangle, shady with its orderly rows of blossoming trees, was the approach to the Mosque of the Caliph (as it used to be) and I was making for the Church of the

Virgin of the Assumption, which now occupies the central part of the vast building.

David and Susanna came only as sightseers, and with good reason, for the place is surely one of the world's wonders.

In Moslem times the blank wall of the mosque was pierced with archways. Through them the ranks of the orange trees were continued by the pillars inside, but the Christians have bricked up the openings so that the effect is lost. Even so, it remains a great marvel.

You step out of the sun-spangled quadrangle with its avenues of living green and gold into a dim, mysterious forest of columns. They say there are a thousand of them, and, as with trees, not one is quite like another. There is pink marble and green, jasper and granite and reddish porphyry, some smooth, some spiral. Instead of foliage, they branch out at the top into arches of white stone and russet brick. Ages ago the infidel ransacked the world for the pillars and collected them in this one mosque. Venture a few paces into the building and you see the endless vistas stretching in every direction. It is easy to fancy yourself lost in a real wood.

At the heart of this maze we came to the small church of the Virgin, dark save for twinkling candles, and with a priest saying Mass for a cluster of kneeling shadows.

'We must part here,' I whispered.

David and his sister murmured their farewells and stole away. I passed behind the carved wood partitions, into the flickering candlelight and the smell of the incense, and joined the other worshippers.

Soon the Mass was over. '*Ite, missa est,*' pronounced the priest. The very words, 'Go, it is ended,' fell on my ears with a second meaning, like an echo. At this moment Solomon was talking to Ibn al Razi. God willing, our mission also was ended, and soon it would be time for me to go, all the way back to England.

I stayed on my knees, while the priest put away the holy vessels and the sparse congregation rustled past me. I prayed for success in this final phase of our venture and for the Virgin's protection on my homeward journey. I vowed to offer candles in the first church I entered after landing safely on English soil.

When I opened my eyes again I was quite alone. Even the priest had taken off his vestments and departed. I stood up, crossed myself once more, and backed out into the gloom of the disused mosque. I hesitated for a few moments, trying to remember from which side I had approached this central Christian enclosure. As I said, it was easy to fancy yourself lost in the dead marble forest. Those infinite avenues looked bewilderingly alike and I felt a spasm of childish panic which I had to fight down with clenched teeth.

'Don't be a fool,' I murmured under my breath. 'Remember how the sunshine slanted in the Court of the Orange Trees? So you came in on the north side of the building. And you know where the east lies, because of the altar. So —'

I started confidently in what I felt sure was the direction of the exit. I had an overmastering impulse to hurry. And to go on tiptoe, though there was now no service to disturb and I seemed to be alone in that labyrinth of arched alleys.

Was I alone? Did it matter, either way? I stole furtive glances to right and left as I went. I am not sure now whether I wished to meet someone or was strangely afraid to do so.

Twice I thought I heard a footfall besides my own. Twice I fancied, as I looked along a fresh vista of columns, that a shadow whisked out of sight behind the soaring marble. Was it only fancy? The forsaken mosque played tricks with echoes and with faint reflections on the sheen of the age-polished stone. And — the uncomfortable realisation rushed upon me — this place, however sanctified now, was originally the handiwork of the infidel, using pillars looted from the heathen temples of the pagan Greeks and Romans. God knows what demons haunted it still.

Suddenly, and this at least was no illusion, a figure in a religious habit stepped into the aisle along which I was hastening. I was quite unreasonably thankful. I pressed forward to meet him, sure that he was one of the priests serving the church. With ten paces separating us, in the self-same instant that I recognised the Dominican robe, I recognised also the pallid face above it.

Zapata!

I stopped in my tracks.

He said nothing. He stopped too, and his right hand came up in a great sweep of his ample sleeve. His fingers clicked. It was like a signal and in the brooding stillness of that place it must have carried some distance.

I turned to the left and ran. But in a moment the empty vista before me was empty no longer. The squat figure of Pierre barred my path, sword drawn.

I swerved to the right. It was like one of those nightmares. One minute the way of escape lay open and inviting; the next — as you had somehow known it would be — it was closed.

Now it was Don Fernando who slipped from between two marble columns and waited for me with wide-flung arms.

He too had a sword.

CHAPTER FOURTEEN

'Meet at the Milestone'

I WHIPPED out my dagger, a Toledo dagger which Benjamin had given me as a keepsake to replace my own. But I should have been mad to measure its short blade against the nobleman's weapon, so I spun round on my heel and fled down another of those glimmering stone avenues.

It was no good. There was another man closing in upon me, a stranger this, but clearly, from his crouching advance and the sword in his hand, another of Zapata's crew.

I zigzagged wildly between the pillars, pausing sometimes to press myself breathlessly against their cold roundness and then to inch my way forward until I could see whether the next vista was clear.

One moment it was Pierre, then Fernando again, then the other man, then the hissed menace of the unseen friar, only a few paces distant: 'This way, you fools! He is this way!'

I felt like a defenceless king in chess, checked on all sides, rushing frantically from square to square to avoid the mate which cannot be staved off forever.

There were too many of them against me. I knew I had no hope of breaking through to the doorway, and by now I had lost all idea of where it lay.

There was another hope, a dubious one. Could I get back to the centre of this eerie labyrinth and take sanctuary at the altar? Surely Zapata and his friends would think twice before committing sacrilege and killing me in the holiest Christian place in Cordova? If I could stay there until the priest returned for the next service, this murderous chess could end, like an ordinary game, in stalemate.

Was it safe to bank on their having such scruples? Men have been dragged from the altar steps before now and butchered like animals . . . Yet, in my desperation, I could think of no other refuge.

I saw, high up between the close-ranked columns, the bead of lamplight locating the screened enclosure where I had just heard Mass. I ran. It beckoned me like some guiding star. And all around me the ancient mosque pattered with footsteps, real and echoed, my own and others, as though the marble forest were whispering with rain.

Zapata must have foreseen my maneuver.

He was there before me, cutting me off from the place of sanctuary, his outspread arms spanning the passage. If he was armed — in disobedience to his religious vows — he made no move to produce a weapon. He was a brave man, I give him that. He calculated that I would not thrust my dagger into the body of an unarmed friar. I might try to shove him aside, but while we struggled his companions would catch up with me.

'Get out of my way!'

My own voice rang oddly, like a stranger's, what with my keyed-up desperation and the weird echoes of the place.

No answer from Zapata. He stayed there, his eyes large and white and staring under his bushy brows, willing me to slacken speed and lower my dagger-point.

From another quarter, though, there was an answer, welcome and unexpected.

133

'*Robin!* Where are you?'

It was David's voice.

'Here!' I yelled. I stopped and set my back against a pillar, ready to defend myself. 'Look out!' I warned him. 'There's Zapata — and Pierre — and — '

'It's all right, we're coming!'

They came, and to my relief there was quite a party of them, not only David and Susanna but Sharada's good-looking young nephew, Daniel, and our borrowed servant, Isaac, from Toledo, all the men with their weapons drawn.

They came down the aisle in a compact little bunch, Susanna in their midst. I glanced back to Zapata, or rather to where he had stood. He had gone. His friends had gone too. Or, if they lurked behind those myriad columns, they judged it best not to turn the affair into a pitched battle.

'I had a presentiment,' said David.

'But — ' I began.

'Home first,' said Daniel Sharada. 'Talk where you can't be overheard.'

We withdrew in an unnatural silence. Of my attackers there was still no sign. Only as we passed into the ghetto did David begin his explanations.

'Father came back, apparently. He asked Daniel to come out and find us. Al Razi is no longer in Cordova.'

'Oh!' I said. My spirits sank with disappointment. Was there no end to this will-o'-the-wisp journey? 'Well, Zapata *is*,' I added bitterly.

'So it seems.'

We entered the house and found Solomon in urgent conference with our host. Susanna broke in with an excited description of the way they had rescued me. 'Daniel was wonderful!' she babbled. I did not quite see why, but there were far more important matters to talk about.

Ibn al Razi had moved to Granada a few weeks earlier.

'I had not heard! I am sorry.' Sharada spread his olive-pale hands in apology. 'Cordova is so big a city. And he lived so quietly.'

Sharada's information services were good enough when he knew what he was after. In the past hour he had discovered that Zapata and Don Fernando had arrived a day ahead of us. Most likely they had taken another route from Toledo. They must have ridden like fury.

'They found us quickly,' I grumbled.

'Easy,' said Daniel, 'if a traveller stays in the ghetto. It needs only a beggar to watch the ghetto gate—and a beggar boy to run with messages.'

'I dare swear I was followed to al Razi's house,' said Solomon, 'but I had my escort. They dared do nothing in daylight in the open street.'

'So,' said Sharada, 'what now?'

'Granada!' David spoke before his father. Solomon heaved a great sigh and nodded.

'I suppose so. Yes, of course. Granada.'

'You will kill yourself, Father!' Susanna objected fiercely. 'You cannot drive yourself to the ends of the world—neither for the Queen's sake nor this Moorish doctor. What do you owe them, either of them?'

'I too am a doctor,' he retorted with a faint smile, 'and it is my duty to save life.'

'Not this way, though,' said Sharada. 'Your daughter is right, my dear Solomon. You are not young enough for this nonsense. You are worn out with this journey from Toledo, you cannot start out on another hundred miles and more—'

'Let *me* go, Father.' David turned and looked at me. I

nodded emphatically. 'Robin will go with me. Give us a letter to al Razi.'

'That's the best thing, Father,' agreed his sister. 'You and I will stay here in Cordova.'

This was so unlike the spirited Susanna that I gave her a quick look to make sure that she was not also showing signs of exhaustion after the journey. Quite the contrary! Then my glance flitted to Daniel, with his splendid eyes and aquiline features, as handsome as her brother — but not her brother.

I realised that Susanna was quite ready to abandon the quest for the Golden Essence and hunt something easier and nearer. I could not help feeling a pang of jealousy.

Solomon let us all persuade him. Speed was vital. He could not outride determined men like those arrayed against us.

'But why,' I asked, 'were they still hanging about in Cordova? Assuming they also know that al Razi has gone to live in Granada, why weren't they already on their way there?'

Sharada smiled. 'You forget one thing, young Englishman.'

'What is that, sir?'

'That Granada is a Moorish city. At peace with Castile, yes — more or less! But these gentlemen from Toledo will not be so free to ride into Granada and arrange matters as they wish. *They* will be the outsiders, the infidel. Even the ingenious Friar Zapata must rack his brains now and consider how he is going to get his way with al Razi.'

'I see. So the most sensible thing was to wait here till we caught up with him and then try to knock us out of the race?'

'Precisely. Once he has done that, he can take his time

and plan the most persuasive approach to al Razi.'

'Then we had best be off,' said David, 'before he tries something fresh.'

Nobody argued against that.

Sharada said he would get hold of a trustworthy Moor, a young man named Yusuf, whom he often dealt with in business, who was now in Cordova and who would do anything for him.

'Yusuf will look after your son,' he assured Solomon. 'He cannot do better than put himself in Yusuf's hands. It will give him a great advantage over these Christians from Castile.'

'How soon can you find him, sir?' David inquired.

'I will send at once. With luck you can be on the road this afternoon.'

Just then one of Sharada's servants came in with a flustered expression, apologising for the interruption.

'What is it, Migash?'

'There is an officer at the gate. From the Alcalde.' That, I knew, meant the chief magistrate in the city — what most Christian nations would call a mayor, but in this and many other things the Spaniards keep the Moorish name.

'What does he want?'

'A complaint has been lodged, Don Samuel. That certain of your guests from England have committed sacrilege in the Church of the Virgin by making an armed affray — '

'This is absurd!' cried Sharada, exploding into laughter. 'What am I supposed to do?'

'You are summoned to attend upon the Alcalde this evening, Don Samuel, and to produce the young gentlemen to answer the charge. Master David ben Solomon and Master Robert of Oxford.'

Zapata had wasted no time. He had not troubled even to discover the names of our companions in the mosque. He was not concerned with Daniel Sharada. His idea was simply to delay us in Cordova by involving us in tedious court proceedings.

Our host saw that as quickly as I did.

'My respects to the Alcalde,' he told the servant. 'Inform the officer that I will attend at the usual hour. And — ' he added, looking straight at Migash and stressing every word — 'that I will speak to the two young men when I see them.'

The servant did not bat an eyelash. He bowed and went out.

Sharada stood up. 'Now we have not a moment to lose,' he said briskly. 'You boys must go instantly.'

'But — the Alcalde?' Solomon looked worried. 'This could make great trouble for you, if you do not produce them.'

'Do not disturb yourself on my account. Migash understood me perfectly. No one will ever know — outside these four walls — that your son and Robin had not already vanished. This is an absurd complaint, anyhow. Daniel's evidence will dispose of it. The Alcalde will not be difficult.' Sharada chuckled. 'He owes me too much money! None the less, the formalities could cost precious days — depend upon it, this Zapata knows the law. The Alcalde will have to listen to a Dominican complaining against a Jew in a matter of religion. No, if the boys are to go to Granada, they must start at once.'

'From what we know of Zapata,' said David, 'he will leave nothing to chance. There will be someone watching the gate of the ghetto.'

'Naturally.'

'Then we shall be challenged and stopped if — '

138

Sharada smiled. 'There are private ways of entering and leaving the ghetto — as my young nephew can show you better than I. The authorities are always telling us, the wall is for our own protection, not to keep us like prisoners.'

'I know three quiet ways of slipping in and out,' said Daniel with a grin, and Susanna gave him an admiring glance.

'But Granada is a long journey,' said Solomon, still worried and rather bemused by the speed with which things were happening. 'They will need fresh horses — I must give them money, compose a letter to al Razi — '

'Not now,' Sharada told him firmly. 'All that can be taken care of — afterwards.'

'Afterwards?'

'Yes.' The merchant turned to us. 'First, you two must get out of the city. On foot. Just as you are. Yusuf will follow as soon as I have organised it. He can bring spare horses and everything you need. Listen carefully. Cross the bridge — it is just beyond the mosque — and follow the road for about three miles.'

'Three miles,' David repeated, nodding.

'You will come to a belt of cypresses. On the left. Look out for an ancient stone at the roadside, carved with Latin names and numbers. It is a relic from the Romans when they ruled in Spain — what they called a "milestone", giving the distances between cities. Wait there. Keep out of sight — the trees will give you cover. It may be some hours before Yusuf can join you.'

'How shall we know him?'

'Oh, he is young, tall, black-bearded, with a turban. He usually rides a grey stallion, one of the Barbary jennets we use so much in these parts. And he will be leading horses for you. If you see anyone like that approaching, show yourselves by the milestone. Yusuf will make himself known.'

Our good-byes were quickly said. Sharada gave us a flask of wine, a loaf and a lump of dried figs to make up for the dinner we should miss. Then Daniel said he would show us a way to slip over the ghetto wall.

Susanna hugged her brother. She said farewell to me much less emotionally, without any of those hearty kisses that English people are so free with, more than any nation I have since encountered. It was certainly not shyness on her part, nor would she have worried too much about David's disapproval. I think that in the past twenty-four hours her interest in me had lessened considerably.

'Take care of each other,' she instructed us, 'and come back safe. Father and I will be waiting for you here.'

I felt quite sure they would be, if the decision lay with her.

Our departure from the ghetto was both simple and discreet. An old tree stood in one of the quiet corrals, those small courtyards serving several houses. Its gnarled grey limbs twisted down to droop over the wall. Daniel pointed to the handiest branch and up we went. It was just a quick scramble amid the screening foliage, a drop and a slither into some lilacs on the other side.

We strolled casually down to the river and then, just as casually, across the bridge. It was immensely long and seemed longer, with the strengthening Andalusian sun hot on our faces and — in my nervous imagination — the eyes of unseen watchers boring into our shoulder blades. Sixteen arches. I counted them, to calm myself. The Guadalquivir is a broad river, two or three hundred yards wide.

No one challenged our departure from Cordova. David had put away his yellow cap — very soon, he said, when we reached Moorish territory, he would be under no compulsion to proclaim his nation and religion by his dress. We looked like any two ordinary youths walking out into the country. After those weeks of travelling in all weathers I was as brown as any Spaniard.

We reached the belt of cypresses before the noonday heat set in. There stood the Roman milestone, a pillar inscribed with the names of the cities and their distances, CORDVBA, HISPALIS, and ILLIBERIS, as the ancients termed Seville and Granada.

'A good idea,' said David; 'we could do with milestones nowadays.'

We stretched ourselves in the shade of those strange trees, pointed and sable-dark, like tightly furled banners. We ate figs, spat out the seeds, and passed the little flagon to and fro. It was really hot now. This Andalusian spring was like an English summer. It was all we could do to keep awake.

Suddenly I felt David shaking me by the arm.

'This looks like our man! A turban, a grey horse, leading two others . . . Come on.'

I scrambled to my feet, blinking in the glare as I followed him to the milestone.

The young horseman drew rein and smiled down at us.

'Salaam!' he said.

'Salaam!' we echoed.

'I am Yusuf. Choose your horses and mount. We must cover as many miles as we can before night.'

We were ready enough. We did not stop even to lengthen the stirrups, but rode off bent-legged as the Moor himself. And so we took the road to Granada, a Christian, a Jew and an infidel, yet from that first moment the best of friends.

CHAPTER FIFTEEN

City Without Bells

'We must ride hard today, and again tomorrow,' cried Yusuf out of his own dust cloud. 'After that — if it is Allah's will — we should be safe.'

Those Barbary horses were ideal for our need. They were smallish and lightly built, but of great staying power and very fast, no good for a knight in armour but perfect for David and me, neither of us yet full-grown men.

David rode a grey named Hamama, or 'the Dove'. That left me with Mansour, signifying 'the Victorious', a bay gelding with white flecks and a black mane that streamed like a pennon in the wind of our passing. A lovely creature . . . I have never ridden a finer, before or since.

Yusuf spoke fluent Spanish and understood ours, but there was not much chance of conversation as we thundered along, usually in single file, with scarves wound over mouths and noses against the choking dust.

We halted seldom, and then only for a few minutes. Yusuf would allow the horses only the merest swallow of water and watched them jealously lest they drank too much. He smiled when David and I seized the first opportunity to adjust our stirrup-leathers.

The Moors cannot imagine why we northern nations ride straight-legged with our feet dangling and not with our knees up as they do. But both parties are convinced that they sit their horses in the only proper way and

neither will ever persuade the other. Yet I am not sure that in this matter, as in many, the Moors may not be wiser than ourselves.

Yusuf knew the road well, the name of each castle on its hill and of each river twining below. His father was a merchant in Granada and often sent him to Cordova on business. Samuel Sharada was a most valued customer, and Yusuf had answered his appeal for help without a moment's hesitation.

We spent that first night as the guests of the headman at a white-walled hill-top village. The people were all Moors, though we were still well inside the territory conquered by Castile fifty years before. They paid their taxes and dues to their new Christian lords but otherwise life went on in the old way.

'Thousands of our people crowded into Granada when the Spaniards took Cordova and Seville,' Yusuf explained, 'but there was not land enough for all. The rest had to choose. They could flee to Africa — or bow their heads to the King of Castile and hope for better days. Who knows?' His sloe-dark eyes sparkled. 'If it is the will of Allah, we may recover this country. There may be caliphs in Cordova again!'

We took supper with the men of the family, sitting cross-legged on goatskin rugs and dipping our right hands into the common bowl. David, I noticed, after a moment's hesitation ate with the rest. As he admitted afterwards, he was not always too particular about observing the Law in every detail. He had done his best to avoid meat in the mixture served us and he knew that there was no danger of tasting pork, since the Moslems also reckon the pig unclean.

Some of their customs, he grumbled privately, were less agreeable. We drank plain water, because the Prophet forbade wine, and we caught no more than a glimpse of the headman's daughters. Ugly old women served the meal. No female sat down to eat with the men or took any part in the conversation.

We slept on rugs spread over the tiled floor of an alcove curving out from the main room of the house. We found that Susanna, bless her, had skilfully packed our saddle-bags with the extra clothes and necessaries we should want for the next week or two.

'And the learned hakim, Solomon, asked me to give you these,' said Yusuf, handing David a bundle of letters and a heavy-looking purse.

Its clink was reassuring. We had rushed away almost empty-handed. However much we could rely on Yusuf, it was good to know that we now had money of our own.

David peered at the letters in the dim lamplight.

'This one is for you, Robin.'

I took it and unfolded it. Solomon had written in great haste, and on paper, which is commonly used in Spain. The Moors make it from plant fibres, and it is cheaper than parchment, and this is one reason why they have so many books and libraries.

It was good of Solomon to send me a note for myself. I could picture him scribbling away against time — one letter to Ibn al Razi, another for his son, a third to a Jewish merchant in Granada who might lend David more money if necessary. And all this while Susanna was packing for us and messengers were seeking Yusuf.

I am grieved that we have had to part in such haste, Solomon had written to me in Latin, *for you know that you have been like another son to me since the day we met in Sherwood. But if God wills that you find al Razi and obtain the Queen's medicine, it is best that you waste no time and run no further risk by returning to Cordova.*

Indeed, it will be wisest to avoid entirely the territories of Castile. Inquire what is best. Don Samuel says you could perhaps take a ship straight from one of the Moorish seaports, like Gibraltar, to Lisbon in Portugal, and thence another vessel to England. If you see the Queen, present my humble duty to her. Let her ask the King why neither David nor I can complete the mission ourselves! No time to write more. David will give you passage-money. God bless you. Solomon.

I passed the paper to David.

'It seems,' I said, and I found my voice oddly shaky, 'that I am not to see your father again — or Susanna.'

'It is best, though.'

'No doubt.'

I looked at my friend, but I could not see his expression, for the lamplight reduced his face to shadowy hollows and a gleam of cheekbone and nose. Did he mean it was best that I should not return to Cordova lest I run into trouble with Zapata — or that I should not see his sister again?

He need not have worried.

'You will need to hurry back to Cordova yourself,' I said edgily, 'or you will miss Susanna's wedding!'

He laughed, but he did not tell me not to talk like a fool.

'I do not think even my determined young sister will get what she wants quite as quickly as that! But I know what you are thinking. I was not blind myself. And it would be most suitable, if Father and Sharada can come to a businesslike arrangement. But if it is not Daniel it will be somebody else. There are so many of our people in Cordova. The main thing is to match her with a boy of our own kind.'

'I am very tired,' I said, pulling a cushion under my

head. 'I am going to sleep now.' I did not, for a long time, but at least I had broken off the discussion.

We were off again at first light, riding straight into a sunrise that flamed up at us from behind the wavy black crest of the hills.

Now we were in the borderland between the Christian dominions and the Kingdom of Granada. Here, a generation ago, the tide of Castile's conquests had reached high water mark An uneasy peace brooded over these marches, often broken by raids and petty campaigns, as happens in the debatable territories between the English and the Scots.

All the castles and watch-towers had the same Moorish look, but for the first few miles, Yusuf explained, they were captained and garrisoned by Christians. At last, when we had splashed through a stony river and were setting our horses to climb the opposite hillside, he said with a smile:

'Good! We can relax a little now.'

'You are in your own country?' David inquired.

Yusuf turned in his saddle and his smile had gone. His eyes flickered angrily. 'It is *all* our country. One day we shall recover it, with Allah's help. But I take your meaning — yes, we are out of the region stolen from us.'

'No offence,' said David with his father's mildness. '*My* people have had no country to call their own for a thousand years.'

Yusuf made a gesture to show that the subject was closed in the friendliest spirit. On the skyline he reined in and glanced back as he had done a score of times. The road behind us, zigzagging down to the ford, was deserted.

'It is good,' he said. He patted his stallion's neck. 'You have done well, Aatik.'

'All your fine horses have done well,' I said. Yusuf's white teeth flashed, and I knew that I had said the right thing.

As we went forward it was easy to see why the Moors boast that their Kingdom of Granada is the garden of Spain.

Had it not been so before, they would have made it so, when the conquering Christian knights drove them into this last and loveliest corner of the peninsula.

Every acre had to be cultivated so as to yield its fullest harvest, and with so many refugees from other parts of Andalusia, there was no lack of willing hands.

All that day we travelled between well-tended vineyards and orchards of orange and lemon. The red earth already shimmered faintly green with the blades of young corn or silver-grey with the olive trees. Yusuf pointed out plantations of mulberry, grown for the leaves on which the silk-worm feeds, and of the tall canes whose sap is honey-sweet and is boiled down into the sugar we import into England at such a high price. And there were fig trees, pomegranate trees decked with vivid scarlet flowers, and many others that I cannot now remember.

Towards evening we were breasting a rise when Yusuf halted and motioned us to draw level with him.

'See,' he said fondly, 'the everlasting snow!'

He pointed. Far off we saw the long sprawl of the mountains that are called in Spanish Sierra Nevada, 'the snowy range'. Mile after mile their upper flanks flashed back the rays of the declining sun.

'Always — always — even in the hottest summer — there is snow up there!'

I wondered why he sounded so pleased. To an Englishman snow is nothing to rejoice over, and the higher the mountain the more horrible we think it. But, as I soon learned, the Moors depend on the Sierra Nevada to keep their rivers flowing during the rainless months. The fertile plain of Granada — the *vega*, as they call it — is kept green only by untiring labour that sends countless rivulets of water racing along man-made channels through the dusty clods. Round and round, endlessly, tramp the patient oxen and horses, raising the buckets to keep up the flow.

Long may the Moors keep the country they tend so well, infidels though they be!

'Tomorrow,' promised Yusuf, 'we should reach the city. And in good time.'

We had had to slacken the killing pace of the first twenty-four hours. Even those hardy little Arab horses could not have kept it up forever, and Yusuf saw no point in driving his beloved beasts to their last gasp.

I think he was somewhat amused by my own anxiety, which I could never quite get rid of.

'This Zapata — this Pierre,' he said. 'They are only men?'

'Of course. But—'

'You speak as though they were afreets or djinns—evil spirits that can fly through the air or change their shapes!'

I answered rather sulkily: 'All I know is that, in spite of everything, we found them in Cordova before us!'

'That was understandable,' David broke in. 'There was another road from Toledo. And we had to ride at Father's pace.'

'I swear to you,' said Yusuf, 'this is the shortest route to Granada. Show me horses that could outdistance these! Forget your fears, Robin. We shall ride into Granada tomorrow. And if these evil men follow us there, let them beware! They are not in the King of Castile's country. This is the realm of King Mohammed.'

He was right, of course. I told myself that. But he had not known the blind terror of that phantasmal hide-and-seek up and down the columned aisles of Cordova. He had not waited for death in that derelict mill above the thundering Tagus.

Travel-weary though I was, I slept fitfully that second night and had uneasy dreams. I was thankful to wake in the grey dawn and hear the muezzin's shrill chant from the minaret, calling the people to prayer. Yusuf was prostrating himself in the direction of Mecca. David put on a skull cap and began his own devotions a little apart. I knelt and mumbled a quick paternoster myself. Then it was time to saddle up and be on our way.

A few hours later we got our first breathtaking view of the Moorish capital, its enormous square red-brown towers seeming almost to float in the heat haze above the level greenery of the *vega*.

'See!' cried Yusuf. 'Did I not promise? Granada!'

The city climbs over two hills, with the steep gorge of

the River Darro between, and this river joins with another greater one, the Genil, rushing down with the snow-cooled water of the Sierra Nevada, which looms in the background all the time.

It is a smaller city than Cordova — even so, it is four times larger than our London — but it gains from its majestic situation, piled up on its reddish cliffs against the blue Andalusian sky. That is how I remember Granada — in bold bright colours, blue sky, white snow, green gardens, and the warm red of the rocks and the walls and those gigantic towers.

The roof-lines of the city were pricked with slender minarets and bulbous with domes and cupolas. There was something strange, and yet not strange, when I thought of it: look whichever way I liked, there was neither tower nor spire to mark a church.

'Is it not beautiful?' Yusuf insisted as we reached the outskirts. The royal citadel — the Alhambra or 'Red Fort' — still seemed to hang in the sky above us, along with the higher quarters of the town. 'You say nothing, Robin! What are you thinking?'

'It is odd,' I said slowly. 'The silence.'

'The silence?'

'I have just remembered — with us, this is a feast day, one of our greatest saints. It seems so strange. This splendid city. Yet not a single bell ringing!'

Yusuf looked shocked. 'By Allah, I should think not! The Koran forbids them. You will find no bells in all Granada.'

'Let us hope that we find al Razi,' said David with some impatience, bringing us back to the matter in hand.

'Amen,' I murmured. And we rode through the outer gate, into that city without bells, and up the hill to the red towers of Granada.

CHAPTER SIXTEEN

The Girl in Trousers

D A V I D and I were determined not to waste a moment.

We refused Yusuf's offer of hospitality at his home: this had been done with infinite tact, stretching our Spanish vocabulary to the utmost, for like most Moors he was proud and sensitive. But I think he understood why we could not rest until we had found al Razi.

It was early afternoon. Though the year was young — at home there would still be frost lining the furrows and few signs of spring — this southern city dozed in the heat. Hardly a voice was heard in the bazaars. The goods dangled listlessly by the dark doorways, carpets and rugs, pots and pans, round shields and curving scimitars with splendidly enamelled hilts, and fine goods of every sort, for Granada is renowned for its craftsmen. But no business was being done at this hour. The traders squatted in the shadowy depths, opening barely half an eye as we jingled along the winding streets.

'The Jennat al-Arif is up the hill,' Yusuf told us. 'A little beyond the Alhambra.'

Our information, passed on by Solomon, was that al Razi had been offered a house there by a Moorish nobleman high in King Mohammed's service.

Yusuf said that this was very likely. The Jennat al-Arif was a small summer palace set in beautiful gardens, which the King preferred to the Red Fort during the hottest months. Various buildings were dotted about in the vicinity, occupied by favoured courtiers. What could be more natural, or more gracious, than to provide quarters there for a learned and honoured physician such as Ibn al Razi, so that he could spend the evening of his life peacefully among the followers of the Prophet rather than under Christian rule?

And how sensible to accept, I told myself as we plodded up the steep road and neared our destination.

Far below, the plain spread like a green tufted carpet at our feet. There was more green above us — yews and cypresses and lilac trees, hedges or clipped myrtle and clusters of spiky cactus — every shade of green from near-black to silver-grey or gold. And everywhere was water, jetting out in tiny fountains, splashing into tiled basins, racing downhill in threads of crystal light. The Moors love gardens and water fascinates them, for their ancestors came from the desert and they can never forget it. On that terraced slope above their city they had created an Eden that Adam might have envied.

This much I noticed and admired with half my mind. But it may be imagined that other thoughts were uppermost during those final minutes of our journey.

Was this really the end of the quest? I dared not believe it until I saw 'the good serpent' with my own eyes.

A gardener directed us. A dozing gate-keeper passed us into a compound, shady with fig trees. He pointed to a simple little house in the far corner. We dismounted. Yusuf led the way up the steps.

A Negro came to the door. He was a giant of a man, bare down to his crimson sash and baggy white trousers. His chest glistened like black armour.

'The Hakim Ibn al Razi? Yes.' How my heart leaped at that one word! 'But the master rests at this hour. Is it urgent?'

'Urgent enough,' said David, moving forward.

The slave still held his ground, filling the doorway under its horseshoe arch.

'There are other doctors,' he said stubbornly. My master takes very few patients nowadays — he is old — he has retired from practice — '

'You are mistaken,' Yusuf interrupted sharply. 'We are not sick. But this young gentleman brings your master an important letter. From Cordova.'

'From Cordova?' echoed a girl's voice. 'What is it, Kafur? What do they want?'

The Negro stepped aside and she came out. I think we were all taken aback. Yusuf must have been shocked because she was not veiled, as decent Moslem women are, though she was fifteen or so and old enough to know better. For myself, the absence of a veil was no cause for complaint. If I blinked it was because she was like no girl I had ever seen in all my travels.

She had the long black hair that is common among the Moors, but her skin was creamy, and her eyes — startlingly brilliant — were as blue as any English girl's. I know now that centuries of intermarriage have made blue eyes and fair complexions common among the Moors of Spain, but I did not know it then.

She was nearly as tall as I was and slender: her gaily embroidered little jacket showed that, though the rest of her was enveloped in voluminous trousers like the Negro's, only hers were overlaid with 'filmy muslin. They ended at small bare ankles and golden-coloured slippers that turned up in front, like her nose.

Yusuf's lip curled up to match.

Undazzled by her beauty and making no secret of his disapproval, he said curtly: 'Young woman, we have business with the illustrious hakim, Ibn al Razi. It cannot wait.'

'It must wait,' she retorted. 'I cannot let my grand-father be troubled until he has had his rest. He is very old and in poor health. *I* have to be *his* hakim!' She laughed. 'But you may come in and wait until the hour is up.'

The Negro led away our horses. We followed her into the principal room of the house. There was a circular pool in the middle with a single jet of water poppling up. She waved us to the cushions that were strewn about the floor. Pointing to an hour-glass she said:

'You see? Half the sand has yet to run. I am sorry, but I must keep to the rules. Kafur!' she called softly to the Negro as he reappeared. 'Bring some refreshment for our guests.'

'At once, mistress!'

David and I had sprawled thankfully upon the cushions. Yusuf remained on his feet.

'You talk of rules, young woman! I must speak my mind before I accept hospitality in this house. Are you not ashamed to show your face like this? To loll wantonly on cushions gossiping with strange men? Is this the way for a true believer —'

She stopped him. She laughed, but there was no offence in her laughter.

'I am sorry. I must explain. By your code I am no "true believer". My mother was a Mozarab — a Christian. So am I.'

Yusuf's manner changed abruptly. 'A thousand pardons!' He flung himself down beside us. 'I did not realise,' he explained to me. 'The young lady is of mixed blood, but of your faith. So it is all right.'

'All right,' said the girl dryly, 'to loll wantonly on cushions gossiping with strange men?'

She remained, I noticed, very primly sitting back on her heels, serving us from the tray that Kafur brought. As her grandfather was a Moslem, there was, of course, no wine. Instead there were goblets of delicious sherbet, fresh fruit juices diluted with ice-cold water. And she offered us nuts and candied sweetmeats from a carved ivory box.

I found my tongue for the first time.

'May we know your name?'

'Of course! Zoraya.'

'A good name,' said Yusuf. 'It means,' he told us, ' "Star of the Morning".'

'I was baptised Clara,' she admitted, 'but I prefer my Moorish name.'

Then we had to tell her ours, and something of our business. We used Spanish, our only common language: Yusuf and Zoraya spoke it almost as fluently as Arabic, David had made great progress in the past two or three months, and I limped along behind the others, grasping most of what was said but keeping rather quiet myself.

It was pleasant resting there in the cool room. Once more I thought how cunning the Moors were with water. The tiny fountain freshened the air and the basin reflected the elaborate coloured patterns of the ceiling directly overhead. Thus one could appreciate their beauty in comfort, as in a mirror, without twisting one's neck to stare upwards.

It was pleasant also to let the eye wander out through an arched doorway at the back, along a narrow vista of lily pond towards a domed pavilion and a pair of cypresses. And no less pleasant to steal an occasional glance at Zoraya, shaking with laughter as David said something to amuse her.

David could be amusing in any language. I swear that he would manage somehow if he had no more than a dozen words of it. It is a matter of confidence. He never lacked that.

'Why!' she exclaimed suddenly. 'The sand has run out of the hour-glass and we never noticed! I must tell my grandfather that you are here.'

Some minutes passed. We sipped our sherbet, scarcely exchanging a word. I felt again all the old tension which the girl's presence had banished for a little while. The tiny fountain mocked us with its incessant burble.

David caught my eye and whispered in English, with a grimace of comical despair: 'I will lay you ten pounds, Robin — our good serpent has chosen this afternoon to die in his sleep!'

I could not laugh. It would be just our luck if he had. 'I would not bet a penny,' I muttered. 'I think we began this journey under an evil star.'

'Well, we are finishing it under a benign one.' He rose gracefully from the cushions. 'Here is our "Star of the Morning". And — if we must speak astrologically — the old gentleman appears to be in the ascendant. At all events, he has got up!'

Yusuf and I leaped to our feet as Zoraya came slowly into the room, her grandfather leaning heavily on her bangled arm.

I had heard so much about al Razi's quietness and humility that I had not expected so impressive a figure. Yet, even in extreme old age, bent and shuffling, he was impressive. He wore a long loose gown of striped cotton, very crisp and clean. His shaven head was bare until Zoraya brought his skull-cap. He took it with a hand that was like a talon. Indeed, with his hooked nose and hooded eyes and sinewy throat he looked just like some ancient falcon, a falcon that was still alert though its wings would never again carry it aloft.

He saluted us with grave courtesy, lowered himself stiffly on to the cushioned ledge of an alcove, and motioned us to recline again. His voice had a slight quaver.

'Your pardon, my young friends. I was studying. This she-dragon who guards my cave will not let me be disturbed.'

I caught Zoraya's blue eyes. They challenged me to betray, for one moment, my knowledge that he had in fact been taking an afternoon nap.

He took Solomon's letter, broke the seal, and read it, holding it almost at the tip of his nose. He took his time, peering fiercely and pausing to rub his eyes. Then he spoke again.

'I remember clearly. One does not forget when it is a queen. And the sister of King Alfonso too. A just man,

Alfonso, and learned, and a good friend to men more learned than himself. A great loss.'

We waited. Old men will talk. But this one came quickly to business.

'It sounds like a return of the lady's former sickness. In which case I know of nothing better than my Golden Essence.' He stared at me. 'You are Robin? You are to take the medicine to England?'

'Yes, doctor. If you will be so kind —'

'Of course! It may take a little while. I treat few patients now, and, as you are too well aware, we have just moved from Cordova. Things may not be unpacked —'

'You know quite well, Grandfather,' the girl rebuked him gently, 'I have seen to everything. All is in order. Nothing lost, nothing spilt or broken.'

'Good, my dear, good. But it is some years since I had occasion to prescribe this remedy. You may have to obtain one or two of the ingredients.'

'What is needed, Grandfather?'

He began to reel off the substances and quantities, but I could not follow the Arabic names. Zoraya nodded intelligently. His eyes narrowed to slits as he strove to concentrate. Then he opened them again and said:

'Wait, my dear. Only a fool trusts his memory in pharmacy. You will find it entered in my prescription book.'

'Very well. I will go and check if we have everything we need.'

I stood up again for courtesy's sake. Al Razi turned at once to David and engaged him in conversation. 'So your father is a physician? And from England? Tell me . . .'

I left David to tell him. Murmuring a vague offer to help, I followed Zoraya into a smaller room near by, which was shelved and fitted up as a dispensary. After one glance over her shoulder she ignored my presence. She took down a well-worn book, bound in beautifully tooled leather, and turned the paper leaves until she found the entry she wanted, inscribed in flowing Arabic script, all loops and dots. Then, with one pink fingernail thoughtfully tapping her parted lips, she ranged along the rows of jars, searching for the necessary items.

I stood in the doorway, shifting my weight from one leg to the other. That small dispensary — sunny and warm and filled with dry fragrances — was a place of beauty and mystery. There was beauty in the jars themselves, for the Moorish pottery is unsurpassed: shapely and lustrous and varying in colour from ruby red to mother-of-pearl and a metallic greenish gold. And there was beauty in the very names of their contents as she murmured them: tamarind and galanga root, cassia bark and dragon's blood, sandal wood and musk and cinnamon, violet sugar and syrup of roses.

Two things, I now realise, were decided in those few quiet minutes, two things that were to determine the whole course of my life since then.

One was that, if I could never be a physician like Solomon or Ibn al Razi, I could perhaps become an apothecary or a spicer and trade in these magical-sounding substances. And the other thing is obvious enough.

She turned suddenly, taking me by surprise, so that I felt my face redden to my hair-roots.

'I can do it,' she said with a smile, 'but it will take three days.'

'Three days! For one flask of medicine?'

'It is an essence, you see. That means distilling. A slow business.'

'You cannot work faster?'

She smiled again. 'Not even for a queen! I am not

working with needle and thread, remember, but with the elements themselves — fire and water and the rest. Nature cannot be hurried.'

'I see.'

We went back to the others and she reported to her grandfather.

'Very well,' he said. 'Three days. Meanwhile, these two young men will be guests under my roof. See to it.'

'As you say, Grandfather.'

She cast her eyes down and turned away, going out quickly, so that I could catch no glimpse of her face.

'She is my hands and my eyes, now that I am old,' said al Razi fondly. 'I have had many sons and daughters — three wives I have had, and my grandchildren are scattered in many cities. Yet Zoraya, the unbeliever and the child of an unbeliever, is the most faithful and loving of them all.'

They must have been talking about Zapata while we were in the dispensary, for David now brought him back to the subject and I could see that he was desperately anxious to make the old man aware of his possible danger.

Al Razi nodded. 'Oh, I know of this friar. He was an ambitious young man at Toledo, haunting the fringes of the Court. He had some grasp of science but he would not follow it with a single mind. No good comes of mixing study with the greed for gold or power.' He gave a contemptuous little snort. 'Just the kind to drop everything and chase after some will-o'-the-wisp like the Elixir of Life!'

'But do you appreciate, sir — he imagines that you possess this Elixir? At any time he may arrive with his precious companions —'

'And do what, my son?' Al Razi looked down on us serenely, sitting upright in his alcove, like some carved prophet in a cathedral. 'This is Granada. This house stands within the precincts of the King's summer palace. There are watchmen and gate-keepers. There is my worthy Kafur whom you have seen — he would break the neck of any intruder with his bare hands. And for the next three days,' he added, 'I shall have the added protection of you and your English friend.'

He made our fears seem very foolish — and what young man likes to appear nervous in the eyes of a much older one? Or in the eyes of a girl? For Zoraya now came back, asking which were our saddle-bags, so that the Negro could carry them in.

Yusuf took his leave, to go down to his own home in the city. We thanked him warmly for all he had done. He smiled and said it was nothing. Clearly he shared al Razi's opinion that all danger was now over.

Zoraya gave us a positive feast that evening. There was a tender young kid stuffed with walnuts, almonds and pistachios. There were different mounds of rice, pearly white and brown and tinted bright yellow with saffron. There were dates and figs and apples and oranges.

For David there was a special dish of kosher meat, which she had somehow obtained from the Jewish quarter down the hill. Ordinarily, it would have been much less trouble for David to use his letter of introduction and stay in the ghetto, but he preferred to accept al Razi's hospitality.

Whether this was, as he put it, 'to strengthen the garrison' or to keep me company for these last few days — or perhaps for some other reason — I was not sure. Certainly his presence added to the liveliness of the household. When I found myself alone with Zoraya I did not know what to say, and when David was with us I had little chance to say anything.

So the next day passed. In the cool of the morning the old doctor insisted on hobbling as far as the Alhambra and taking us into the citadel. It was very splendid, with courtyards and flowers and fountains everywhere, but I enjoyed the evening still more, when David kept al Razi company and Zoraya took me to see the gardens of the Jennat al-Arif itself.

We watched the sun go down over the plain below, its last rays flushing the long white slopes of the Sierra Nevada.

'Look at the evening star,' she said. 'Like a jewel!'

David would have laughed and said something clever about preferring the morning star, but I had no skill in paying compliments. The rhetoric a clerk studies at Oxford is small help when he has to deal with girls.

'Supper,' said Zoraya quickly. 'Grandfather likes to eat soon after sunset.'

Another evening passed, and the night, and another day. In the dispensary the alembic bubbled softly and the fragrance of orange rind crept into the living room. Drop by precious drop, the golden liquid dripped down the long glass neck into the flask clamped ready to receive it. Every hour Zoraya went in to tend it. Every hour brought nearer the moment of my departure.

It was all planned. Yusuf came up and helped to make the arrangements. He had business for his father in Malaga, the principal port of Granada and an easy journey from the capital. He would escort me there and set me on a ship bound for Lisbon.

David used his father's letter of credit to draw money for his own needs and mine. He gave me enough gold dinars to cover all foreseeable expenses on my homeward voyage. It was agreed that, if the Queen rewarded our efforts with any further payment, I would do my best to transmit a half share to David in Cordova.

There was little else to do but write letters to Solomon and Susanna. The second letter proved easier than I had expected. I saw now that I had never been in love with Susanna — I had not even known what love was. It had simply been that a pretty girl is always a challenge, especially if her brother keeps emphasising that she is out of bounds!

I hoped she would be very happy. I did not say 'with Daniel Sharada', but I was fairly sure that she would get her way. I felt much less certain of my own future. It hung before me as a particularly depressing blank.

At supper the old doctor smiled at me and said:

'So — we have only tomorrow, my young friend. And the next day you must leave us?'

I looked at him in surprise. 'No, sir, it is tomorrow I have to go.'

He shook his head. 'That is not possible. Zoraya says there is not yet a flaskful of the Golden Essence. You cannot offer a half-empty bottle to your Queen! And, having waited so long, she can doubtless wait one more day.'

'I have already told Yusuf,' said the girl, 'and he says it will suit him better. He has to organise a whole train of mules to carry his goods to Malaga.' She was bending over the supper dishes and her face was hidden by her long black hair.

'So be it,' I said. 'The day *after* tomorrow, then.'

At that moment I became aware of an odd and frightening phenomenon.

I have described how we reclined on the tiled floor around the shallow pool and how the water (hardly ruffled by the one small jet) served to mirror the elaborate decorations on the ceiling high overhead.

It had another effect also, if you lay on the right side of it. Without turning your head to look through the open archway and down the long garden vista, you could — from some angles — use the pool to frame a reflected picture of that view. The Moors are most cunning in these devices.

A bright crescent moon had risen between the cypresses at the far end of the long straight pond. It glinted on the black surface between the clusters of sleeping lilies. And as I peered into the marble basin at my elbow, curious to see how much of the scene outside was caught in its reflection, I let out an exclamation under my breath.

'What is it?' cried Zoraya, alarmed.

I leaped to my feet and peered out into the garden. I was shaking.

'I could have sworn it — '

'What?'

'That Pierre — the Gascon I told you of — was out there, watching us!' I pointed. 'Up there — on that little balcony under the dome — '

'You saw him? But — '

'In this pool — reflected!'

'There is no one there,' said David soothingly.

'Reflections play curious tricks,' quavered al Razi.

Just then there was a mighty hubbub at the front door. Kafur came backwards into the room, protesting loudly. Suddenly the whole place was full of men. Drawn scimitars flashed like moons in the lamplight. A respectful voice was apologising to al Razi in Arabic. In Spanish, and in a high-pitched voice I knew, I caught the words:

'There are the two young men. I can identify them!'

Zapata had changed his black robe for a nobleman's dress, but the face staring at me in triumph was unmistakable.

CHAPTER SEVENTEEN

Final Settlement

My arms were gripped by two powerful Moors, and a razor-sharp sword waved discouragingly under my chin.

David, I could see, was equally helpless. Al Razi was pouring out questions and complaints in agitated Arabic. Zoraya stood wide-eyed with horror.

Some kind of Moorish official was striving to reassure them. He turned and beckoned. Zapata stepped forward with a bow. Don Fernando followed. The officer introduced them, using Spanish as a matter of courtesy, and the conversation continued in that language, so that I could now glean some idea of what was happening.

'Learned hakim,' said the officer, 'these gentlemen have just arrived from Cordova. They say that these two youths have been in trouble with the authorities there, and there is reason to believe that they have come here with the intention of swindling you.'

'Absurd! They are my guests!'

'Many a good man has entertained scoundrels unawares — and paid a heavy penalty for his innocence.'

Al Razi answered breathlessly, and Zoraya laid a restraining hand on his arm. She was clearly anxious that he should not make himself ill. But he flung off her hand impatiently.

'These — *gentlemen* — they are the scoundrels! I have been warned against them.'

'Naturally,' said Zapata in a smooth tone, 'the young

men came to you with a well-prepared story. They knew that Don Fernando and I were aware of their intentions. So they did their utmost to discredit us. We understand, and excuse your discourtesy.'

'We make allowances for an old man,' put in Don Fernando ungraciously. 'As a grandee of Castile I am not used to being called "scoundrel". But I can see that Ibn al Razi has been imposed upon. These youths are very glib.'

'This is utterly outrageous,' said David. 'There are other respectable people in Granada who can speak for us — both Moor and Jew. We brought letters — '

'Forged,' said Zapata.

'And Don Samuel Sharada will vouch for us in Cordova. Send and inquire there — you will find that the charges were falsely trumped up against us '

'But you admit that there *were* charges?' demanded the officer swiftly. He had been looking very embarrassed and unhappy. He pounced on David's last words. He turned to al Razi. 'This is extremely difficult, learned hakim. It cannot be sorted out tonight. In the morning these young men must be brought before the magistrate. Then you can speak in their favour, if you wish, and they can call other witnesses and try to establish their innocence.'

'We shall, sir, do not worry,' David assured him.

'In the morning?' objected Zapata. 'What if the birds have flown? What if you find this trustful old man with his throat cut?'

'I am not a fool,' said the officer tartly. He addressed al Razi. 'I regret this, learned hakim, but I cannot take the responsibility of leaving them here overnight. I must take them into custody.' Al Razi began to protest again and upset himself so much that he had to sit down.

Zoraya brought a cup of something and tilted it against his lips.

The officer seized the opportunity to withdraw.

'Do not let your grandfather fret,' he assured her in a kindly tone. 'If our suspicions are wrong, all will be cleared up tomorrow and no harm done. If it proves otherwise, he will be grateful to us.'

'Very well,' she said. 'But — treat them well.' She looked over her shoulder at him and I saw the pleading in her eyes. 'If there are expenses — I mean for their food, drink, anything — I know that my grandfather will pay.'

'Have no fear, young lady.'

And with that they dragged us away. The last things I heard were Zoraya's words of encouragement shouted after us and then the thud of the heavy outer door as Kafur banged it and shot the bolts.

Somewhere on the road downhill Zapata and Don Fernando wished the officer good night and went their way. He saluted with respect and told them the hour and place they must attend tomorrow, to make good their accusations. There was peace between Granada and Castile just at that time and I could not blame a minor official for treating a Castilian nobleman with deference.

I had no chance to speak to David until we reached the lock-up a few minutes later. I fancy it was a place where petty criminals and disorderly persons were kept safe until they could be dealt with. It was no more than a tower with barred windows and a single jailer, who grumbled sleepily as he came forward to take delivery of us.

It was a cheerless building, bare and smelly. A cheap oil lamp burned on a high ledge, revealing the mat on which the man had been dozing, the remains of his supper, and a flagon which — to judge by the fellow's strong breath — did not comply with the Prophet's ban on alcohol.

The remainder of the ground floor was taken up by two cells, partitioned from each other by a brick wall but open to view in front, like animals' cages. Through the bars of one I saw several hunched figures. They stirred. Curious eyes peered out at us from under unkempt hair.

The jailer was going to unlock this door and put us in with them, but the officer murmured something and we were pushed into the empty cell instead.

'I have told Ali you are to be treated well,' he told us. 'If you are really innocent you have nothing to fear. There is justice in Granada.'

He wished us good night and left. The jailer locked up and stretched himself on his mat again. I turned to David.

'Well?' I said despairingly.

'There'll be trouble about this,' he promised, inspecting our quarters with disgust. He was indignant, but not as concerned as I had expected. 'Don't worry,' he went on. 'Al Razi will get on to Yusuf in the morning — and Sharada's friends in the Jewish quarter — and — '

'Yes,' I broke in. 'Tomorrow! But what do you think is going to happen tonight?'

He looked at me uncomprehendingly. 'We shall be deplorably uncomfortable in this hole, we may pick up fleas or worse, but — '

'I'm not thinking of *us*. Al Razi! And Zoraya. They're alone in that house except for Kafur.'

'I know that. But they're on their guard now. They won't open that door tonight to anybody. And remember, we made sure ourselves there's no other way to get into the place.'

That was true enough.

On our first day we had made a quiet inspection of the

premises. It was a typical Moorish house, presenting a blank face to the outer world. Without a battering ram, which would have wakened the whole neighbourhood, no one could enter unless the door was willingly opened to him.

We had not neglected to study the garden at the back. The walls looked low, but when we scrambled up and peered over we saw that, because of the mountain slope, there was a formidable drop the other side.

'Yes,' I said, 'but we agreed that *if* you had a confederate inside, to drop you a rope ladder from the garden terrace — '

'Kafur wouldn't do a thing like that! He worships both of them.'

'I wasn't thinking of Kafur. Did you see Pierre leave the house with us?'

'I never saw Pierre at all. He wasn't there.'

'I tell you he was,' I insisted desperately. 'I swear it. He was looking at us from the end of the lily pond, just before the others rushed into the room. Don't ask me how he got there. Perhaps he slipped in through the front door while Kafur was arguing with the officer. Anyhow, he didn't come away with Zapata and Fernando.'

David let out a groan of dismay. 'Then — if you're right — he's still there! And if the other two go back he can find some way to let them in !'

That was the thought that had been torturing me. If Pierre could settle the Negro, Zoraya and the old man would be utterly defenceless. Anything could happen before morning, and here were David and I, not half a mile away, but unable to help.

It was the only explanation that made sense of Zapata's behaviour. Merely to give David and me an unpleasant night in the local jail, knowing that we should win our release the next day, was far too petty an objective. No, his plan was to get us out of the way so that he could reach al Razi — and, as he imagined, the secret elixir.

David started to pace up and down. 'We've got to get out of here!'

'But how? Can you work miracles?' I gripped the cold iron bars until my hands felt bruised. I could have spared myself. Prison bars are not made to be bent by boys.

'We can offer this fellow money. Pray God he understands something besides Arabic. Ali!' he called softly. Grumbling, the jailer rose from his mat and came over.

He understood quite enough Spanish to realise how many gold dinars David was promising him if he would release us. His battered, rather unintelligent face was a study of mingled disbelief and greed. The very thought of so much money made him dribble — but how could he trust us? And how could he escape terrible punishment if he did let us go?

David had sometimes told me, cynically, that money would buy anything if you had enough of it. He found that he was wrong that night.

Ali spat contemptuously, told us to be quiet, and went back to his mat, taking a swig from his flagon to console himself.

'Sottish ape!' muttered David. 'I wish I had my father's medicine chest — I can think of a few things I would like to mix into his wine.'

So could I. But it would not have helped us, whether the man was drunk, drugged or dead, if his keys had still been hanging at his girdle and ourselves still locked behind the bars. Nor would a pound of pepper have been any use in this case.

'Oh, if your father were here,' I said idly, 'I suppose he could cast him into a deep sleep without any drugs — as when he took out my aching tooth that day and I knew nothing — but if he could not also bewitch the fellow into opening the door — '

'Stop!' David hissed. His face was transformed even in that dim light. 'Let me think . . . let me think . . . you have given me an idea.' He stood there, tense and concentrating. It was as though his thought were a captive bird, fluttering and striving to escape. I did not dare to interrupt him. But after a few moments he pulled me down beside him on the bench which ran along the wall and began to explain.

'It may not work,' he whispered, 'but it can do no harm to try. You remember how Father drew your tooth? Well, I cannot draw teeth or set bones, but I can — sometimes — put people to sleep as Father can.'

'*You* — ?'

'I have done it several times — just for amusement. Only with Susanna. A sort of game. I saw no other purpose in it. You cannot cast such a sleep on a person who consciously resists it. But — this is the point — if he *does* yield to it, you can give him instructions which he will obey without thinking, once he wakes again.'

'You mean you could tell a jailer to set you free?' I demanded, husky with awe and excitement.

David shook his head. 'It is not so simple. The sleeper will not obey all instructions. Not those that offend his sense of right and wrong. When I played this game with Susanna I could make her pick up one of Father's books and open it at a certain page — but if I had told her to throw it out of the window she would not have done so. Father says that divine providence watches over such sleepers when they wake, so that they cannot be bewitched into sin. Otherwise, you could use innocent men to commit murders.'

My spirits sank.

'How does this help us? How can you put the man to sleep if he does not wish it? And even then, if you cannot make him do anything he regards as wrong — ' I laughed sourly. 'He has already shown us that he considers it wrong to let us go.'

'It is worth trying,' he insisted, 'but it has got to be done delicately. Fortunately he understands Spanish. And I think there is enough light.'

'Light?'

'I could not do it without light. You remember in your own case? It helps if there is something bright for the eyes to fix on. I am going to call him over again. Keep in the background and don't utter a word. He mustn't be distracted.'

After our previous attempt to bribe him, Ali was reluctant to bestir himself, but at last David's whispered appeals brought him to the bars. He kept his distance, though. A jailer must quickly learn not to stand too close to his captives.

David was talking in an urgent yet soothing undertone. He held up a dinar, turning the golden coin this way and that. Ali's eyes followed it greedily, in spite of himself. But I heard him grumble:

'I tell you it is useless. More than my life is worth. Why don't you go to sleep — and let me?'

'You shall sleep in a little while, Ali. You shall sleep when I have counted ten. But tell me first: how many of these dinars would you take as a free gift? One? Two? Three?'

I remembered Solomon's voice all those months ago in Nottingham. His counting had been my last recollection before I awakened to find my toothache gone.

By 'ten' the Moor was standing rigid with glazed eyes, sound asleep.

David was still talking. It was uncanny. I wanted to cross myself, but it might have broken the spell. And whatever ungodly powers David was invoking, I admit I did not want it broken.

'You are asleep,' David told him in that strangely compulsive undertone. 'You understand all I say, but when you wake you will remember nothing. When you wake it will be morning — you will have overslept — the officer will be waiting outside, angry and impatient. Someone will say, "You are late, Ali." Then you will not waste a moment — you will open the outer door and then you will open this cell and walk in. The prisoners must be ready for the officer.'

I could see the sweat on David's temples, a narrow gleam outlining his silhouetted profile. He was putting all his strength of will into dominating the unconscious jailer.

'I shall count five. At "five" you will wake up. You will remember nothing. But you will do as I have told you. One, two . . .'

And it was so. At 'five' Ali twitched, moved his feet, and looked round him with a bemused expression. I held my breath.

'You are late, Ali,' said David.

Instantly the man broke into panic-stricken activity. He rushed to the door, unbolted it, and pulled it open as though he had heard furious knocking outside. Then, without a backward glance, stammering apologies and fumbling with the keys at his belt, he fairly ran towards our cell. The lock clicked, the gate groaned as it slid sideways.

My hands were raised, but David made a warning gesture. There was no need to use violence. As the flustered Moor came in, we simply slipped out behind him. A few moments later we were outside in the moonlight.

'It would have been cruel to lock him in,' said David. 'He will be wise to vanish before the guards arrive, or I hate to think of his punishment. This is something he will not be able to explain!'

'Can *you*?'

'No! I scarcely dared hope it would work, even. I remembered all that Father had told me and did my best.'

It had worked, that was the main thing. For the moment we were free. We could go back to al Razi's house. But — this was the doubt that tortured us — should we be in time?

It was still the middle of the night. We were unarmed — yet where could we turn for help? We dared not lose vital time by waking up people in the Jewish quarter or trying to find out where Yusuf lived. We panted up the hill in the clear silver light, praying that we should meet no patrolling watchmen. To our relief we saw only a scavenging cur that bared its teeth at us from the shadows.

'The outer gate — ' I stammered. 'We shall have to wake the porter — and if he knows that we were arrested — '

'We must take a look round first. We may be lucky. But if we have to wake the porter we must chance it.'

I soon saw what was in David's mind. If Pierre had let down a rope ladder to his masters it might still be there, left hanging for their return journey.

It was fortunate that we had studied the lie of the land so thoroughly in the daytime. David led the way confidently along a weedy path stinking of garbage. Another stray dog snarled at us and resumed its foraging. We found ourselves in the scrubby ravine into which we had once looked down from al Razi's garden terrace.

'Yes,' he said softly.

It was a relief, yet at the same time alarming, to find a ladder of thin strong cord trailing down over the soft cushions of creeper and clinging fern, just about where we had expected it.

David went up first. I followed. We pulled ourselves over the parapet and dropped silently onto the tiled path beside the lily pond.

There was a lamp still burning in the main room of the house. Pierre was clearly visible. He stood with his back to us, broad-shouldered, squat, hands on hips, filling most of the archway. From beyond him came the murmur of voices.

David pressed my arm. 'Can we get our swords?' he breathed in my ear.

'We can try. We must.'

They should be where we had left them, with the rest of our few possessions, in a small guest chamber opening straight onto the garden. It was part of one wing. The other wing contained the dispensary and the rooms where al Razi and Zoraya slept.

They were certainly not asleep now.

As we crept forward, measuring our soundless paces with infinite care, Zoraya's cry rose high above the other voices.

'Do not touch him! He is old!'

That cry was just what I needed. I forgot fear, ceased to count the odds against us. Again David pressed my arm, restraining me from hasty movement.

As we drew nearer we could see past Pierre's jutting elbow. Zoraya was being held back by Don Fernando. Al Razi lay sprawled on the cushions as though he had been roughly thrown there. Zapata bent over him in a menacing attitude. Of Kafur there was no sign. No doubt Pierre had silenced him long ago.

We reached the door of our bed-chamber. David held

aside the bead curtain so that its swish should not betray us. Thankfully we slipped into the sheltering gloom. We groped for our swords and eased them from their scabbards, inch by cautious inch. It was good to wrap one's sweating fingers round a solid hilt.

'Pierre first.' David's whisper was all but soundless. 'Leave him to me. Do not move till I do.'

Once more that lifting and lowering of the bead curtain . . . once more the tiled terrace under our feet, the all-too-brilliant moon, the babyish purling of the tiny fountain, too soft to muffle an ant's footsteps, let alone a man's . . .

Pierre *must* not hear us. Nor his companions see us, stealing up behind him out of the night.

They seemed intent on what was happening in the room.

'Stop lying!' That was Zapata, scowling down at al Razi. 'We know you have the elixir. Have you given those young men your formula?'

'How could I?' Weak though it was, the doctor's voice had lost none of its dignity. 'I tell you, there is no such thing as the Elixir of Life. It is a fool's dream—'

'Naturally you say that! But think: it is hours till daylight, hours before we shall be disturbed. You might well talk now. We shall not leave without the formula.'

'Kill me if you wish.'

'How would that help?' demanded Zapata crudely. 'But perhaps this girl is another matter. To save *her* from harm, I fancy you might reconsider your decision!'

'Are you scholars or animals?' Shaken out of his calm fortitude, al Razi tried to struggle upright. Zapata threw him back on to the cushions. Zoraya screamed; Pierre and Don Fernando laughed.

This was our moment. David straightened himself and stepped forward with upraised sword. I followed.

Like myself, David had never had any training in arms. He would have been handier with a dagger. As it was, though Pierre reeled away from the stroke, gasping with pain and surprise and splashing the doorway with blood, the wound was not mortal. In no time he was staggering back into the fight, cursing and howling like a demon.

Zapata turned to face us. His jaw dropped. For a moment even he was thrown off balance.

'How in the devil's name — ' he began. Then he slipped nimbly behind al Razi's outstretched figure and whipped out a short sword himself. 'Never mind,' he said between his teeth. 'We can kill all the birds with one stone.'

Don Fernando had released his grip on Zoraya. She fled from the room. That was not quite like her, but I do not know what she could have done to help us or her prostrate grandfather.

So it was two to three, with Pierre all the more dangerous because he was wounded. And though the friar may have been as untrained a swordsman as we were, our other two opponents were skilled in arms. Luckily, in such moments, there is no time to calculate your chances.

'Kill them,' said Zapata quietly, as though he were ordering dinner. He stood back while Pierre lurched forward to attack David and the young nobleman advanced to deal with me.

Our swords clashed together. As I felt my whole arm tingle under the impact I knew that his strength would soon beat down my guard. I gave ground, thinking to retreat round the curved rim of the fountain. David also was being forced back by the Gascon's murderous assault. And out of the corner of my eye I could see Zapata hovering, alert to stab either of us from behind.

His opening never came.

Suddenly Kafur came hurtling through from the kitchen quarters. I compared the wounded Pierre with a howling demon, but there are no words to describe the infuriated Negro. Blood caked his wiry hair, cut cords flicked from his wrists and ankles, his face was a living gargoyle of berserk rage.

Zoraya was at his heels, whirling a heavy staff of al Razi's. There was no need of her; there was no longer, in fact, much need of David and myself.

Kafur took Zapata with his bare hands and before any of us could utter a word he had — there is no other word for it — broken him. I heard the terrible snap of the bone. Zapata sprawled and lay still, like a man tossed by a bull, his oval face impossibly askew upon his shoulders.

Fernando broke off his attack on me, spun round and raced for safety in the garden. Pierre — professional to the last, never taking more chances than the money justified — was prompt to follow him. But not quite prompt enough. David struck out at him; he seemed to stagger as he reached the long lily pond. Then in he went, shattering the reflection of the moonlight.

Kafur went after Fernando. He reached the rope ladder and unhitched it when the nobleman was still swaying half-way down the wall. I learned later that Fernando escaped with a broken ankle and a thorough bruising.

Zoraya and I fell on our knees beside al Razi. She cradled his head. His eyes were closed.

Behind us, David said: 'Pierre is dead. Kafur has just got him out of the water. And Zapata too. He died quicker than he deserved!' Then the fierce triumph in his voice faded. 'How is the doctor?' he faltered.

Zoraya lifted her head and looked at us with swimming eyes. Even if she could have spoken, there was no need.

CHAPTER EIGHTEEN

Charing Cross

'It was his heart,' Zoraya told me afterwards. 'Sometimes it was like a fluttering bird. Dear Grandfather, he warned me not to be frightened if some day Death took him suddenly.'

It was a few days before I could leave for Malaga and start my long journey to England. Ibn al Razi had to be laid to rest according to the rites of Islam, about the magistrates of Granada had to be satisfied about the strange doings of that night.

This proved easier than we expected. Zoraya and Kafur testified that the two dead Spaniards had broken into the house, caused al Razi's death of shock, and been killed in lawful self-defence. It was confirmed that David and I had been guests and had acted to protect our host. Don Fernando had fled, presumably back to Castilian territory, and he did not put in an appearance to complain on behalf of his late friends.

The one tricky point was our own arrest earlier the same night, and our quite inexplicable escape from the jail. Nothing was said about this to the magistrates. Perhaps the officer concerned did not want to confuse their minds. It seemed to be a matter best forgotten in the interests of everybody.

No doubt it helped also that we had Yusuf and his influential father on our side, and the Granada Jews to whom Sharada had given us letters of introduction.

As David remarked sagely, 'When the authorities want to close an embarrassing case they begin with a little closing of their eyes!'

Other problems were harder to settle.

'What will happen to the girl?' said Yusuf when he came up to tell me the revised plans for our journey to Malaga.

'It is difficult,' said David. The three of us were sitting by the lily pond, watching the lizards scuttle across the tiles. 'She has no family or friends here, of course. I have offered to take her back to Cordova, but she seems unwilling. They left Cordova because they were not happy there.'

'She is old enough for marriage. But is there money for a dowry?'

'Not much. Al Razi may have been a genius at medicine but he was a fool with money.' David could never quite forgive a man who was that. 'The house, of course, did not belong to him: he was offered it rent-free by an admirer. He leaves little cash, just the household chattels they brought with them. Kafur is to be given his freedom. And I must say that he deserves it, though he is a very valuable slave.'

'Nothing else?' asked Yusuf. 'The books and drugs?'

'Ah, yes! They are worth something, certainly. I should be glad to make a fair offer for them on my father's behalf. But,' David added, turning to me, 'you must realise that those drugs aren't worth a tenth here of what they would fetch in London. They are common here. In England some of them are rare, even unheard of.' His eye brightened. 'That gives me an idea, Robin. Why not do Zoraya and yourself a good turn? *You* buy the lot at Granada prices — and take them back and set up shop in London!'

'A fine suggestion,' I said sarcastically. 'How long

before I was put to death as a poisoner? I don't know what half of them are!'

Though I laughed off David's proposal, I see now that his words must have pushed me a little further along the way I was fated to go. Since meeting his father I had become more and more interested in medicine, and especially in the healing power of drugs. Al Razi's dispensary had been a revelation to me. These Moors had a skill in pharmacy unknown to the apothecaries of England.

'She is a beautiful girl,' said Yusuf thoughtfully, 'and virtuous, for all that she goes unveiled in the house and talks freely with us men. It would help if she would turn to the true faith —'

'She will not do that,' said David. 'She says your religion teaches that females have no souls.'

'True!'

David laughed. 'Can you see Zoraya giving up her soul — even to win a husband?'

'Well, mixed marriages are common enough — like her own parents' marriage. But the lack of a dowry does not help. I wonder —' Yusuf stroked his beard. 'I wonder what my father would say.'

'Your father?' I exclaimed, startled.

'Yes.' Yusuf sounded remarkably casual. 'I have a wife and two small daughters, but no son as yet.' I never recalled his mentioning these facts before. 'My father does not wish me to take a second wife until I am thirty and have made my own way in the world. Perhaps if he saw Zoraya . . .'

I did not like the way the discussion was tending. I made an excuse to leave them and went into the house. I heard Zoraya moving about in the dispensary.

'Here is your Golden Essence,' she said. 'It is packed carefully, see, so that the bottle cannot get broken. It

183

would be a pity, after all you have gone through to get it.'

'Thank you, Zoraya.'

She was so serene and competent, now that the first shock of grief was over. Each day I realised more and more what a strong character she was — not self-centred or demanding, but with al Razi's calm integrity.

'Well,' she said, 'you three have been very busy settling my future.'

'We have settled nothing. That is what troubles me.'

'Troubles *you*?'

'Naturally.' And it seemed natural enough. We had known each other so short a time but much had happened. 'The day after tomorrow,' I said, 'Yusuf is taking me to Malaga. David will return to Cordova. You will be alone.'

'God will take care of me.'

'No doubt! But God expects His children to help in the work!'

'You need not worry about me, Robin.'

'How can I *not* worry?' I answered irritably. 'Here you are, orphaned, alone, homeless, a Christian girl in a Moslem kingdom — '

'Go on! Add that I have no inheritance to buy me a husband!'

'I did not say so.'

'But it is the truth. I am a nobody, the most hopeless kind of nobody. Who would possibly want to marry me?'

'*I* would.'

The words burst out without my meaning to say them. Her back was turned to me as she moved the drug jars on the shelves. She did not answer or wheel round to face me. I dared not stop to think how she had taken my declaration. Nervously I gabbled on:

'I have no right to ask you — I have even less than you have — I am even more of a nobody! I have no craft or trade. Unless I win the Queen's favour with this essence, I have no prospects. I am not clever or good-looking like David — '

'Robin!' She swung round, but the window was behind her and still I could not see her properly, though I think she was smiling. She was a shadowy outline, with the sunshine glinting on her hair like a halo, and all those coloured jars shining red and green and gold. 'I believe you are jealous of David!'

'You are always talking to him — he makes you laugh. I cannot blame you if you prefer David, but — '

She took a step towards me, raised her hands and gripped the folds of my tunic, shaking me gently as a mother might shake a child, for all my extra inch or two of height.

'Prefer David? Dear Robin! For an Oxford clerk you can be *very* stupid. Whose shoulder did I cry on when I saw that Grandfather was dead?'

After that, things arranged themselves with unbelievable ease. There is one advantage about being a nobody: if there are two of you, you can marry without anyone's interference.

True, I was very young to take a wife, and I know that today my worthy neighbours in Cheapside look doubtfully at a sixteen-year-old bridegroom unless he has a father well established in the business of the City. But (as I reassured myself at the time) Zoraya and I were a few months older than Queen Eleanor and her Edward when they went to the altar to begin their long and happy life together. So that is *two* ways in which we followed the royal example.

Poor Queen! I often wonder if the Golden Essence would have restored her to health. But at least all the delays and misadventures of our Spanish journey made no difference. When we landed at Southampton in April we heard the news that had long been stale in England: the Queen had died in Nottinghamshire at the end of November, long before we reached even Toledo. Without wings of magic we could not possibly have saved her.

The King was for a long time heartbroken. He had splendid memorial crosses set up to mark each place where her coffin had rested on its mournful progress southwards to Westminster Abbey, where my own children's children can still gaze upon her effigy and know from the carver's art that I did not exaggerate her beauty.

When Zoraya and I arrived in London the workmen were setting up the last of the memorial crosses, not a mile from the Abbey itself, between Westminster and the city itself.

'*Ma chère reine,*' Edward had called her in the French tongue, 'my beloved queen'. Since then the Cockneys have twisted his words in their own fashion, and they call it 'Charing' Cross.

We stood looking at it sadly that first time, a grey drizzling day in early summer.

'So good-bye to all hopes of royal favour,' I said. 'We shall always be nobodies now.'

Zoraya touched my hand stealthily. No one saw. 'I do not mind, Robin.'

The rain fell faster. 'Are you sure you are not pining for the red towers of Granada?'

'What do *you* think, Robin?' she whispered back.